I0451729

The Non Adventures of

Alice the Erotic Author

by

Ava Manello

ISBN-13:978-0993243615 (KBK Publishing)

ISBN-10:0993243614

First published 2017 by KBK Publishing

Dedication

This book is dedicated to all the erotic authors out there who have to live in their imaginations, and to the readers who live vicariously through them.

The Non Adventures of Alice the Erotic Author

Introduction

There's an element of Alice that is autobiographical, however, it's not the fantasies; they're a product of a healthy and vivid imagination. Damn shame, I know.

There's poetic license in here and an awful lot of fiction, the only character based on a real person is Alice herself.

The books that Alice writes are centered on the books that I have written as Ava Manello; so you may see an insight into how some of the characters and plot lines developed.

Prologue

I've barely slept all night. Now I've made my decision I can't put it off any longer. The torment is killing me. The decision was years in the making, but it was the right decision. It's my choice alone, although I suspect he won't see it that way.

The alarm clock isn't due to go off for another hour, but right now that's no good to me. Shaking him awake I utter the words that will split us apart.

'I can't do this anymore.' My voice breaks, and I'm angry when I start crying.

'I want a divorce.'

The words are finally out, the words I've kept trapped inside for longer than I can remember. There's no going back now.

Chapter One – Six Weeks

Later

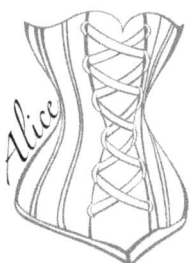

The front door closes and I let out a sigh of relief as the last of my visitors leave. Silence reigns throughout my little bungalow, and for the first time in my forty-five-years I'm on my own. Don't get me wrong, I'm not asking for sympathy, it was my choice. Taking a deep breath I pull my shoulders back and stand straight.

'You can do this,' I reassure myself.

I'm optimistic about the future, and I feel like a huge weight has finally been lifted from my shoulders. Turning back into the sparsely furnished living room, I take in the garden chairs that are my seating for the next few weeks until the sofas arrive, the TV stand that's currently bare, the empty corner unit, and the cold electric fireplace with its empty mantle. The nest of coffee tables is littered with empty fish and chip paper and dirty coffee cups. For once I don't care, it's a reminder of the support I've had from family and friends who helped me move today.

I gather up the detritus and move into the tiny kitchen. The dark worktop and black appliances complement the light oak doors of the units. Filling the sink with hot, soapy water, I wash the mugs and cutlery. The sink is under a large window, which shows my rear garden in all its weed-infested glory. The sun is just setting, casting a warming glow despite the overgrown vegetation. I dry the pots, putting them away and enjoy the clean, uncluttered kitchen for a moment.

The important things are in place; the Wi-Fi was connected before I moved in. I take a fresh coffee with me, settle into a garden chair, and pull up the furniture store on my iPad. Time to order a desk for me to write at now I know how much space I have to play with. It would be nice to order a couple of bookcases as well.

The silence should seem odd, there's no blare of the TV, no constant interruptions, and it's comforting. I wriggle once again in the chair, after all the lifting my back is aching. I decide to head to bed despite the early hour. I can't wait for the sofas to arrive.

The bedroom greets me with warm pine and crisp white Egyptian cotton bedding. It's my sanctuary. I ignore the wall of boxes under the window, deciding I'll finish unpacking tomorrow. Picking up my iPad I open the Pages app and read back over the chapter plan for the book I'm writing. The release date is just thirty days away; I can't believe that in just a few short months I've released my first book and am about to release my second. Common sense tells me I should have postponed the release with everything that's happened, but I ended the first book on a cliffhanger and even I can't leave my readers hanging like that.

I can't seem to focus on the words so I put the iPad down for a moment. Everything feels so surreal right now. Six weeks ago my life was very different. Then I asked for a divorce. I can't quite grasp that any of this is real. Four months ago I never dreamed I'd be an author, never mind living a whole new life to boot.

I wonder how long it will take to get used to my new home. Right now it feels like an escape, similar to staying in a hotel, a temporary reprieve from my miserable existence, but a life I'll have to return to. I pinch myself, thinking this must be a dream. Damn, that hurt. This shit is for real. I can't stop the huge grin that lights up my face at the realization.

I've left almost everything behind and started afresh. All the furniture and appliances are new, it's just clothes and books and bits and bobs that I've brought with me. I've never lived on my own before; it's exciting and uneasy at the same time. For so many years I did what was expected of me; putting aside my hopes and dreams to endure the life I thought I had to lead, rather than the one I wanted to live. Now is my time to shine. One of my friends said I was having a mid life crisis, I prefer to think of it as a late youth rebellion.

Aside from continuing my writing there are things I want to do, get a tattoo for one (when I've decided on the image I want), and learn to ride a motorbike for another. I want to dye my hair bright colors, although right now I'd just settle for covering the grey. I'm even contemplating a piercing, although I need to give a lot more thought to that one.

Right now, the future's mine. I can't wait to see what it has in store for me!

Chapter Two – The Episode

With The Spider

It's only been a few days, but I've learned one of the pitfalls of living on your own. There's no one else to get rid of the spiders!

I've had arachnophobia for as long as I can remember; even small spiders see me running from the room. The beast that shared my bathroom this evening was far from small, I recognize it as a wolf spider. If you don't know what that is, just imagine a spider with long legs that's almost the size of the palm of your hand. I don't care what it's called right now though; it's a bloody squatter. As I'm paying the rent on this house, it's getting evicted.

Don't ask me why my eyes were drawn to the side of the toilet u-bend, I've no idea. I'd gone into the bathroom to answer a call of nature and nearly wet myself in fear. The offending beast was sitting there large as life on the bathroom wall, half hidden by a water pipe. I looked around the bathroom, finding nothing suitable in reach. With my back to the wall and my eyes on my uninvited guest I slicked my way into the kitchen. Nothing! It comes to something when the only thing suitable to deal with a spider is a wooden spoon. I had nothing longer. Picking up a can of fly spray as back up I braved my way back to the bathroom. He was still there. I shuddered.

Edging closer as slowly as I could my eyes never left the interloper. My whole body was braced for even the slightest hint of movement from the eight-legged monster. The handle of the wooden spoon suddenly felt way too small, I would have been more comfortable with something six foot in length that shot flames and electrocuted the little bugger.

I shrieked as a leg showed signs of movement. My whole body was on edge and my heart was beating as though it was trying to escape my chest.

'Listen you little fucker!' I screeched. 'I'm paying the rent here and there's no room for lodgers.' I hissed. Turning the fly spray on him, I gave it my all.

Now normally fly spray is a choking but fine mist. Not when you aim most of a can at an Olympic record paced spider as it races around the bathroom wall towards you. No, when you have it on almost constant spray it kind of turns into foam. I'm not sure if the spider started suffocating, but at least he started to slow down just as he came to the radiator I was cowering next to. Before he made it to the safety of the rear of the radiator I let loose with the wooden spoon. I beat that little fekker to death. I have no shame over this; I don't care if it was one of God's creatures. At that moment in time - it was him or me.

I looked down at the wooden spoon in disgust. That would have to go in the bin, along with the squished remains of my unwanted visitor. Now, if you're a fellow arachnophobe you'll understand that it couldn't go in the kitchen bin. That was far too risky, despite his squished and very dead state, there's that part of you that still believes the little sod will come back to life in the night and come and get you! With that in mind I opened the back door, raised the bin lid and disposed of the spider spoon with haste.

I rushed back into the house, slamming the door behind me and checking it was locked. My skin was still crawling at the thought of what I'd just seen and experienced.

When I finally stopped shaking, I gave myself a mental high five; I'd just survived my first spider.

Chapter Three – The

Burlesque Show

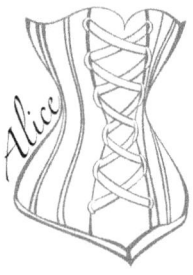

My new desk has arrived and I love it; it almost matches the rest of the oak effect furniture in my living room. It's solid and looks expensive, although it was actually on sale in the DIY store. I may have accidentally dropped a couple of bookcases in the online shopping basket as well.

My MacBook laptop looks perfect on it, and my comfy leather effect chair is far more comfortable for my aching back. Goodbye garden chairs.

I had a huge grin on my face earlier as I built the smaller bookcase on my own. I used my own toolkit. I'm proud of my toolkit. I went for a sensible blue one rather than the girly pink one. My brother and his friend don't like my toolkit, they take the piss out of it as they walk in with their cordless drills and powered screwdrivers, but whose toolkit was needed when they wanted an Allen key? Mine! They can diss it all they want, it's one of my best investments since I moved in on my own.

The desk and large bookcase were a two-man job, but I was the second man so am equally as proud of those. For years I wasn't allowed to do anything DIY. It had been that long since I'd done anything like this that I began to feel I couldn't, that's what happens when people tell you that you can't do something.

It's a constant drip of criticism that saps your confidence and self worth. It's so subtle you don't see it happening, until one morning you wake up and don't recognize the person you've become.

Enough of dwelling on the past, this is my new start. I'm rather excited about going to review a Burlesque show tonight, the flyer said there's a prize for the best costume and I'm pretty pleased with mine.

I've never been to a burlesque show before, so I'm not really sure what to expect, but I do know that burlesque celebrates curves, and I have curves in abundance; although I kind of lack the rhythm to actually go to a class. I'd contemplated pole-dancing lessons until I saw the bruising on someone on YouTube who'd tried it.

The outfits are so sensual. I had great fun choosing mine, although budget dictated something on the economy side as it's only for one night. Some of the costumes were amazing with sparkles, frills and ribbons, but so were the prices.

Dunking another plain chocolate digestive in my coffee I let my imagination run away with me.

The burlesque club is dimly lit, a haze of smoke hanging just below the ceiling, the crystal of the chandeliers sparkling as the flame effect lights reflect against the cut glass. I make my way over to the bar where I'm meeting the manager for my interview. I'm nervous as this is something outside my comfort zone, but I'm confident that I look the part. My generous bust almost overflows the confines of the tight red corset, and my skintight leather leggings coupled with five inch black heels make my legs look as though they go on forever. I've a lace choker with a red stone sitting just in the dip in my throat, and a tiny black hat with lace and a red feather clipped in my hair. I haven't got the rhythm to apply for one of the dancing roles, but I sure know my way around a club and am here for a bar tending position to supplement the recent slump in my book sales.

There's only one person sitting at the bar, his back is to me, but I can see by the taut pull of his suit jacket across his shoulders that he's well built. The kind of build that comes from hours in a gym. I lick my lips in nervous expectation just as he turns to look at me. The click of my heels on the laminate wood floor must have caught his attention. Damn, he has the most piercing blue eyes, and as he smiles in greeting my heart almost bursts out of my chest. I'm definitely an eyes and smile girl, and this guy has an enchanting smile. I falter, lost for a moment in sinful thoughts of what I'd like to do with him, and he steps away from the bar stool, reaching out a hand to steady me.

'Are you okay?' I can hear genuine concern in his voice. I can't quite place the accent, but it's definitely northern and sounds sexy as hell.

I let out a nervous laugh in response, 'I'm fine, thank you. It's just a while since I wore heels.' I apologize.

He looks down at my heels, slowly moving his eyes up my body, taking in my long legs, passing my waist before pausing rather longer than needed on my bust. I silently pray he doesn't look too closely at my arms; they definitely need some toning up. I'm at that age where they resemble chicken wings and flap around in the wind. I let out a sigh of relief when he moves beyond them and gives me an appreciative nod.

'They look good on you,' he compliments me. 'Come and take a seat. It's Alice isn't it?'

I settle onto the high but comfortable barstool, my nerves quickly disappearing as we engage in friendly conversation. We seem to talk about everything but bar work.

'Can you start this evening?' he asks out of the blue. He hasn't even interviewed me yet, how can he be offering me the job?

'Don't we need to do an interview?' I query.

The laugh he makes has my lady parts throbbing, it's so sensual. Damn, I'm pretty sure I've just blushed traffic light red. Let's hope he thinks it's in response to being offered the job rather than being turned on.

'What do you think we've been doing for the last hour?' he chuckles.

Fuck, I clench my thighs even tighter together. Has it really been an hour? The conversation had flowed so easily I'd lost track of time. Disappointment rears its ugly head; here I was thinking we had a connection whilst he was just conducting business. It slowly sinks in that I've got the job though and a grin lights up my face.

'You mean I got the job?' I squeal. Now I blush even harder, Goddam it, I sound like a bloody teenage girl rather than the mature woman I am.

'Yeah, I think you'll be good for business,' he smirks at me. 'We do have a few rules though, no

fraternizing with the customers, you can accept a tip but no drinking on the job, and you've got to be on time.'

That all sounds easy enough. I sigh as I realize that no fraternizing probably extends to the other staff as well. At least I'll have a bit of company; it can be a quiet, lonely life sitting with just a laptop for company even if it connects me to my readers and friends on social media. I decide to brave the question anyway.

'What about fraternizing with the staff?' I almost whisper.

'That depends.' His tone has changed, he sounds disappointed with my question.

'On what?' I ask, sounding far too eager. I need to calm myself down.

'On which member of staff you were wanting to fraternize with.' He pauses and looks at me.

'Erm, I, erm...' I stammer out. I hardly think it's appropriate to tell him I'd like to fraternize with him, but can't think of the words. What a time to get writers block. My nerves are shot, my pussy is doing my thinking for me right now and that's never a good thing, especially when I'm in the middle of a job interview.

'And just what you class as fraternization.' He winks at me. He bloody winked!

I'm out of my comfort zone now, big time. He starts to rise from the stool and I'm left almost slack jawed as his t-shirt stretches across his taut abs. Somewhere during the interview he'd discarded his suit jacket revealing a tight black v neck that flatters his physique. It's obvious he spends time in the gym. You don't get a body like that eating McDonalds that's for sure.

He offers me his hand and I rise hesitantly, I glance back at the chair hoping I haven't left a wet patch from all my sexual excitement. I let out a silent sigh of relief when I spot no marks, amazed as I was sure I'd been wet enough to cause a deluge.

'Let me show you round, follow me,' he invites.

Oh yes, I'd follow him anywhere. I catch myself, hoping I haven't said the words out loud. He gives me a puzzled look, but I think I'm okay. He's probably wondering why I haven't moved to follow him so I rush to catch up. Stumbling on my heels I start to fall. Crap, I'm about to face plant when a strong hand grabs my arm and steadies me. The rush of heat when his hand connects with my skin shocks me for a moment. He pulls me closer to his chiseled chest and draws me in close. I could get arrested for the dirty thoughts I'm having right now, but make no effort to step away. I could get used to this.

'Are you okay?' Déjà vu flows through me as he repeats the words from earlier when I stumbled coming in, this time though I'm sure I hear more warmth in them, and genuine concern.

'Yes, thank you. I'll practice wearing the heels a bit more, I'll be fine.' I try and laugh it off, but I'm not sure it comes across as confident as I wanted it to. I can hear a hint of mania in my voice.

'I've always had a thing for a woman in heels,' he confides with a wink. My stomach does a back flip. 'They are pretty killer heels,' he grins as he angles his head in their direction.

He steps back, but keeps his hand on my arm to guide me. We tour the bar area first, and he shows me where everything is stored and how the tills work. I'll be given a plastic key tonight that's programmed for me. It means that we can all use the tills, without having to wait for the other staff to log out. I've used one in the past. The scale of the bar is bigger than the ones I'm used to, and definitely better stocked, but nothing I can't handle. I won't be expected to mix cocktails as they have a dedicated mixologist. That's a relief, as my memory of the recipes is sketchy at best.

Behind the stage there's a discreet door that he leads me through once we've finished inspecting the bar. The corridor behind it is dimly lit, but clean and uncluttered.

'This leads to the offices and the dressing room,' he offers.

The dressing room is the first one we come to, it looks like an explosion of color when we open the door. There are spangles and feathers everywhere I look, although it's neat and tidy albeit full.

The wall in front of us is covered in mirrors with lots of lighting. Damn, I thought a hairdressers mirror was unforgiving, but this is worse. There's no hiding any flaw in that. The worktop under it is festooned with vibrant colors of make up, sparkling jewelry and nipple tassels. I've always been fascinated by nipple tassels, though never brave enough to try them.

As we turn to leave the room his hand trails over a red leather flogger on the worktop, his fingers caressing the braided handle. Absentmindedly he picks it up before turning and leading us from the room. I'm almost frustrated when he closes the door behind us, the room was so interesting and the skimpy costumes and vivid colors had my imagination working overtime.

He opens the next door and I'm startled to see someone in the office. He introduces her as Jenna, his PA, who handles the payroll and HR stuff as well. After he's introduced me he lets her know that he'll bring me back later to complete my paperwork. I'm slightly disappointed to know we're not alone in here, but then I shouldn't be surprised that there are office staff working during the day.

Further along the corridor there's a storeroom. There are glass chiller cabinets for the white wines and beers, a fancy store for the red wines and bottle after bottle of spirits. This door is locked with a key card, and only the head bar staff have *access. I can understand why, there must be a small fortune in here. It's a fascinating room.*

The door at the very end of the corridor is isolated from the others, when it opens it reveals a well-appointed and very masculine office. The large oak desk is larger than my dining table! The chairs are rich black leather and look extremely comfortable, but not quite as comfortable as the luxuriant black leather sofa that takes up most of one wall, and is big enough to sleep on. There's a clean masculine smell to the room that I can't quite place, it could be cedar or sandalwood, and perhaps a hint of musk. Whatever it is, it's pleasant.

He heads to the chair behind the imposing leather desk and gestures to one of the seats in front. I sink into the rich black leather, I could get used to this. Reaching into a drawer he pulls out a black plastic wallet and removes a sheaf of papers. He explains that this is the employee pack I'll need to complete, as well as containing the clubs code of conduct for employees.

He hands me a matte black Cross pen to complete the forms with. There's nothing cheap about anything in this place; everything exudes class and style. It's a beautiful pen to write with and one of my favorite Brands although I do prefer a fountain pen for things like this. There's something special about watching the ink form the letters on the page. I think it looks more thoughtful as well. You can't beat a thank you note handwritten with a fountain pen.

He excuses himself, checking his emails on his sleek Apple MacBook whilst I work my way through the employee pack. I now have Apple envy, as it's clearly the newest model, much thinner and sleeker than my trusty machine. I look up from the bank information form, wondering what's caught my attention, to see him absentmindedly playing with the flogger he brought from the dressing room. Every time he releases the mouse from scrolling through his emails his fingers caress the flogger. I'm not sure if it's just my age but it suddenly seems awfully warm in here!

He notices my attention and pauses. 'You're interested in this?' he questions. My mouth suddenly goes dry, how do I respond?

I chicken out and just nod my head in agreement. He picks up the flogger, almost examining it as he responds. 'This ones just a cheap prop, it looks good from a distance, but it's nowhere as good as the real thing,' he advises.

I sit upright wanting to pay attention and know more, pushing my shoulders back in the process, which inadvertently causes my already ample bosom to become more pronounced. He smirks, but I'm sure I detect a hint of approval in there.

'You can get different types depending on what you want, they can be soft if they're made from rabbit skin, perfect if you want sensual instead of sting. Deer leather feels soft as silk and has a light thud but hardly any sting. The other extreme like oiled leather has a very pronounced sting. No two are quite the same. Have you ever tried one?' His

look is piercing as though he can see deep into my soul.

There's no point in lying to him, I sense that he would know. I still can't get any words out so gently shake my head, no. I can see I've piqued his interest now.

'Would you like to try one?' His voice oozes sexuality and I want to shout out loud and tell him yes. But no, this is me we're talking about, so I blush from my bust to my forehead and give an almost imperceptible nod instead.

He rises from his seat and moves around the desk towards me. I gasp at the picture before me, his tight t-shirt, well fitted trousers and the flogger in his hand have me almost salivating.

'You do know that a flogger shouldn't be used on an arse don't you?' he asks softly.

I shake my head no; it's news to me.

'The best tool for that job is a paddle,' he explains. 'A flogger is more sensual; it's about the sensation rather than the sting of a slap. If you don't know what you're doing you can do some serious damage with a flogger.'

By now he's standing beside me, turning the flogger in his hands as he talks. His hands are level with my breasts and I crane my neck back to look up at him, just as he trails the ends of the flogger across my chest. My nipples strain against the tight confines of the corset.

'A flogger is for teasing, trailing along the skin. It should be as light as your lovers touch.' He continues.

To be honest I'm not sure I need a flogger, his voice is doing it for me on it's own. All the time he's talking to me he's trailing the ends of the flogger along my arm, causing goose bumps to rise on my skin.

'These tails are actually called 'falls' and they can cause the most amazing sensations on your back if used correctly.' If I thought I was wet before, I think I have Niagara Falls in my knickers now!

The flogger is tracing circles up my arm and he draws it across my bust again. I want to combust. The trail moves round my neck and starts to caress my naked shoulders. A shudder of pleasure runs through me. I'm so turned on and he hasn't even touched me yet. If this cheap flogger feels this good I can only imagine what his preferred model would feel like.

I feel the loss as the flogger leaves my skin. Instead he turns the handle and places it under my chin, applying just enough pressure to lift my head so I'm looking into his crystal blue eyes. I could get lost in them. Between his soft-spoken voice and those eyes, I feel almost hypnotized. Right now he could ask me to do anything and I would.

His soft fingers reach down into my corset and find a nipple; I shiver as he tweaks it roughly. The sensation is amazing. My hand reaches out and brushes against the obvious bulge in his trousers. I'm rewarded with a twitch from his impressively sized cock, and I hear him gasp. My eyes don't leave his as I reach for the fastening on his trousers. A strong hand grabs my wrist, pausing my action.

'Are you sure?' he queries. I can hear the desire in his voice and it would be rude to disappoint him.

'Mm hm.' I whisper, shaking off his grip.

Using both hands I unfasten his trousers, drawing them down his thighs. He's wearing tight black boxers, his erection straining for release. I tease my hand over the soft material covering him. He groans in approval and I continue my exploration, teasing him through the material and feeling his already stiff cock further harden at my touch.

When I've teased him to the point his pre-come is seeping through the material I ease the boxer briefs down as well. He has a magnificent cock. This is a cock worth writing about. My hand caresses his soft silky length; I can feel the vein pulsing beneath my touch. I draw my polished nails from his balls to his crown and relish the shiver that runs through his body.

Bravely I reach around, placing my other hand on his pert and firm arse, pulling him closer to me. Pumping him gently with one hand I caress his arse with my other. Every so often he releases a moan of satisfaction, which empowers me to continue with my exploration.

His cock feels so soft against my hand but I need more, I need to taste him. I lick my lips in anticipation and his cock jumps in appreciation. I don't draw him into my mouth just yet, instead I lean closer and swirl my tongue around the tip, teasing the pre-come and tasting the saltiness of him, before running my tongue along the underside of his cock. I kiss and gently nip my way down his length, slightly daunted by his size. I'm a little concerned I'll choke on it, if I'm honest, but the temptation to taste him is more powerful.

Running my tongue back up his length I once again tease the tip, circling a couple of times before drawing him fully into my mouth. He drops the flogger he'd still been holding and let's out a loud groan of satisfaction. His words are mumbled, but the tone is one of intense gratification. That's good enough for me. His hips move slowly at first, almost as though he's scared of hurting me, but the more I caress his cock with my mouth the more he moves, thrusting gently into my mouth. I almost gag at one point, but adjust my position so his length is away from the back of my throat. My hand continues to pump and I can feel when he's about to come. His posture becomes more rigid, his balls tense.

'Stop.' He groans, almost sounding pained, 'I'm going to come.'

He tries to move back but I increase my grip and take him further into my mouth, increasing the pace of my hand. He lets out a mighty groan as his seed spills down my throat. Even when he's finished, his cock is still hard. I take my time licking and sucking, cleaning every last drop of come from him before releasing him and sitting back in my chair, licking my lips in satisfaction.

His legs seem to lose strength and he collapses back against his desk. 'Fuck,' he gasps. 'That was outstanding.'

I grin. I can't help myself.

He returns my grin, and there's a devilish twinkle in his eye. 'I think I need to return the favor,' he gestures to the couch. 'You need to get those trousers off.'

Just as my fantasy is about to get really interesting the alarm sounds on my laptop, reminding me of the time. Bugger, I've managed to lose an entire afternoon to my writing. It's time for me to get ready for the burlesque show.

It's not the warmest of nights and there's a hint of rain in the air. I draw my thigh length mac more tightly around me as I totter on my heels towards the theatre. Normally at this hour you can see the build up of the audience as they head to the theatre but foot fall seems lighter than I expected. As yet, I haven't seen anyone else dressed up. My friend looks at me, concern in her eyes, and I can tell she's thinking the same thing as me. We've made a mistake.

I haven't gone for the outfit in my fantasy, instead I've gone more traditional. That and the trousers were a bit on the tight side when I tried them on. I blame the chocolate digestives. I've gone with a purple ruffled burlesque skirt cut short at the front and long at the back, paired with a boned black corset that has sparkling diamanté around the bust. Add a pair of kick ass heels and black stockings that make my legs look like they go on forever, a perky little hat with lace, I think I definitely look the part.

The bar area of the theatre is empty apart from three couples in jeans and sweaters. I look around in confusion, have we got the wrong night? We walk through the bar, trying to be as inconspicuous as possible as we make our way to the box office where I'm supposed to collect our tickets.

The cashier explains that the show isn't starting till 8pm, rather than the usual half seven. That's why it's so quiet. Letting out a breath of relief we decide to go sit in the bar and kill time that way. There are a few more people than before, but still no one in costume. I draw my coat a little tighter and hope no one notices.

Having expressed silent outrage at the extortionate cost of the drink, we find a dark corner to hide in. It would have been much cheaper to go to the pub across the road for an hour, and if I hadn't been dressed like this, I would have done.

The time passes quickly as we catch up, not having seen each other for a few months. As the bar fills up I've yet to see anyone else in costume. I look across from me and sure enough there's the poster with the fancy dress competition along the bottom corner. I didn't get it wrong after all.

At eight pm we're in our seats in the balcony, and to my horror we're the only two in the theatre in burlesque. I've seen a few women arrive in vintage outfits, the billowing fifties skirts or form fitting dresses with the beehive or lacquered large hair, but nothing as extreme as us. Oh well, at least I didn't come on my own.

The curtain rises and I'm drawn in by the show. The glamorous hostess in her stylish and bejeweled

1920's style ball gowns, the corny guy with his hula hoops and ten curvaceous burlesque dancers who I'm delighted to see have cellulite. They're not thin, they have curves and tattoos and boobs, and I love it.

There's laughter aplenty when one of the twirling nipple tassels become loose and flies off into the audience, landing neatly on an old mans lap. I make a mental note not to try nipple tassels after that.

 The show is a delight, very entertaining and well performed with only one problem. There's no fancy dress competition. Now I feel really stupid and embarrassed at my outfit. It's the wrong thing in the wrong place at the right time. When I left home I felt sexy, now I feel shamed. I try and hide in my coat. My friend tries to persuade me we should just shrug it off and head to the pub – a few drinks will soon rectify this. She's right; I'll feel much better when I've had a Fireball or two.

But that's when the Alice curse strikes again. The problem with being a writer who walks round the house barefoot all the time is the lack of practice in heels. As we head out of the door I'm eye flirting with the hot bouncer over the road at the pub, trying to ignore the smirk on his face when the wind blows my coat open and he spies my outfit.

Just as he laughs and nudges his colleague to look at us, the inevitable happens. My heel catches in the uneven pavement. I hear the crack of the heel just as my balance gives way and I land face first on the cobbled road. When I finally make it upright – it took both bouncers to lift me back up - I'm left with holes in my stockings and bloody knees the like of which I've not had since I was a toddler.

I've barely made it upright before a passing drunk lurches into my face and laughs at me.

'Can't you handle your drink, love?' He's still laughing as he staggers off, too quickly for me to slap him.

I've had enough. Brushing aside the bad jokes and curious glances from passers by, I limp to a waiting taxi and head to the comfort and sanctuary that is home.

So much for an erotic burlesque adventure!

Chapter Four The Bicycle

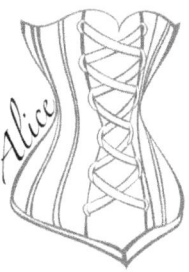

Now my grazed knees have abated I really need to think about getting fitter. I guess the stress of the last few weeks has shown in my waistline as I'm the slimmest I've been in years, but now I'm in a bungalow and working from home I need to do something.

I've been looking for a second hand bicycle to use for those trips to the supermarket where you only want a few things. So far nothing has taken my fancy. I'm checking online when a sale grabs my attention. There's a basic woman's bicycle that I can buy with some vouchers I have and they can deliver it in two days. It doesn't have a basket on the front, but I can soon buy one of those and fit it myself. I decide to go for it, despite the fact I've hardly cycled in the last 20 years and it tends to bugger up my knees.

I used to cycle from one side of town to the other every day. I've cycled with guitars and pasteboards on the handlebars. I've cycled down the side of traffic. I did everything without fear back in the day. What changed that? I got my driving license and realized how suicidal cyclists can be. I much prefer the safety of my four wheel box, but I'm a realist. Taking the car to the supermarket that's only fifteen minutes walk away is both lazy and wasteful.

I place the order.

Two days later my shiny new bicycle arrives. In a flat pack box! I wasn't expecting that.

Never one to be phased I decide not to call in help and resolve to tackle this project on my own.

I'm a grown woman, how hard can it be!

It soon becomes apparent that a native speaker has not written the so-called 'English' instructions. I try and follow the images as best I can, but they're hardly conducive to success.

An hour later I stand back and admire my work. It certainly looks like a bicycle. I fit the basket I picked up yesterday. Now comes the acid test.

I mount the bicycle and slowly wobble down the driveway. Mmh. The handlebars need tightening. Once fixed in place I try again. That feels better. The driveway isn't long enough for me to get enough speed up to avoid wobbling, and I live on a busy road so I decide to brave the slightly quieter side street.

You know the saying 'you never forget how to ride a bicycle'? It's not quite true.

I sway along the street, having to stop and put my foot down for balance every few yards. Something's not quite right. I head home and inspect the instructions again.

Whilst I have the handlebars facing the right way, the front forks are back to front. Pfft. Half an hour later with the forks fixed I try again. To be fair it's not much better, it looks like a case of operator error rather than mechanical.

The only thing for it is practice. I'm going to attempt a foray to the supermarket!

Having secured the cycle helmet on my head I grab my purse, phone and keys and set off.

It's a good job the basket on the front doesn't have a swear jar fitted. I'd be bankrupt before the end of the first street. The roads around where I live are riddled with potholes. You'd think the bloody things were breeding. On a road that's the width of two cars I'm forced to cycle more in the middle than I'm comfortable with. Couple that with parked cars blocking the road at intervals on both sides and I'm conscious that I'm holding up traffic behind me with my slow pace.

I come to the first obstacle, a T-junction. Thankfully I'm turning left. I come to a stop to watch for traffic and almost lose my balance. Not the most auspicious start. I've barely turned the corner before the next challenge. A mini roundabout.

I pull to the side of the road and consider my options. I need to take the second exit, which means turning right with the potential of cars coming at me. I take the only suitable option. I dismount and cross the road at the pedestrian crossing, and once at the other side, cross again till I'm back on the side of the road where I need to be. Phew. I'm coming out in a hot sweat already, and it's not that warm a day. I take off my cardigan and fold it into the basket.

The supermarket has a side entrance for pedestrians and cyclists. I'm so grateful as it means I won't have to tackle the huge roundabout. I weave between the parked cars until I come to the bicycle rack, and dismount with relief. I'm practically gasping for breath and obviously don't look like I'm doing too well as a fragile looking old lady toddles over to offer assistance.

'Are you okay, dear?' She sounds concerned. 'Do you need me to go get a first aider for you?'

I'd answer her, I really would. I just can't get my breath at the moment. I try and gesture that I'm okay and she looks even more anxious.

'I'll....' huff, 'be,' huff, huff, 'fine,' I offer weakly.

'Out..of...practice,' I finally get out.

'Well, if you're sure?' She doesn't sound convinced, but thankfully leaves me to my own devices.

It's another ten minutes before I get enough breath back to actually venture into the store.

Carrying my small bike basket in my hand like a trophy I head inside.

The problem with this particular supermarket and me is I'm like a magpie once I enter. I'm drawn to all the lovely shiny things that I didn't actually come in for. I look at the minuteness of the bicycle basket in disgust, and decide that this is a challenge I can fully embrace.

I should tell you I only came here for bread and milk.

Three quarters of an hour later I leave, my basket full of things that I didn't need, but desperately wanted as soon as I saw them. It's only when I start to unpack in my kitchen at home that I realize I forgot both the bread and the milk.

Damn. I do the only sensible thing in the circumstances and walk over the road to the minimart opposite. In hindsight I should have gone there in the first place. It would have saved me a fortune and the potential heart attack.

I need another solution to getting fit.

Chapter Five Male Strippers

Tonight is all about research. Well, that's my excuse. I'm off to see some male strippers at the local theatre. It's all in the name of the new book that I'm writing, of course. After all, there's a limit to how many strip shows you can watch on YouTube.

I've not been to see a male strip show in over twenty years, and I can't say I was all that impressed back then. I'd made the mistake of sitting on the end of the aisle and had been pounced on by one of the performers. He'd strutted his way from the stage to my seat. All the time I sat there thinking, 'Please, not me,' whilst everyone around me was wishing the opposite.

With a sinking heart I saw him stop at my side. He was wearing the tightest, tiny black pants. I know this because he thrust them into my face when he straddled my lap. I'd like to say he filled them out, but I can't. Instead I almost choked on the odor. I knew these guys oiled up but it smelled offensive. The scent was grimy and dirty as though he hadn't washed in a week, and was mixed with fake tan. Pretending to smile, I endured the humiliating encounter; inhaling a breath of fresh air when he moved on to the next willing participant.

Safe to say that's not going to happen tonight - I've booked the dress circle.

I've followed this particular group on Facebook, and I'm hopeful that it's going to be a good evening. They're a large national troupe that has regular permanent shows in several large cities as well as this touring entourage.

We're going to the pub across the road from the venue for a meal before the show. I'm with my Mum and her friend. When we arrive the tour bus is already outside the theatre. Tanned torsos and abs adorn the side of the vehicle, floor to ceiling. It looks pretty impressive.

Before we've finished eating we've had a taste of what's to come. A few tables behind us there's a gaggle of women talking at the top of their voices about what they'd like the strippers to do to them after the show, and discussing the sexual merits of several of their past encounters. It's not complimentary, let's put it that way. They come across as brash and bawdy. If it had been men having this particular conversation they'd have been asked to leave by now. I'm actually ashamed to be in the same side of the bar for fear I'll be associated with them. It's one thing thinking about sex, I make a living out of that after all. Even having a private and quiet conversation with a friend is fine, but it's something else when you're discussing it at the top of your voice in a pub for everyone to hear. It's disrespectful to the person being talked about.

When we get to the show it's pretty much more of the same, the majority of the audience are like the women from the bar. At least it's given me some great ideas for character development for the audience scenes in the book

The show starts with a bang, literally. A huge crash of music heralds the arrival of the strippers on stage. It soon becomes apparent that these guys are new. They're out of sync, lacking in rhythm, and look nothing like the bodies plastered across the side of the tour bus.

The number finishes and the stage goes dark. We sit there, and sit there, wondering what's happening. Rather than have an act fill the space whilst the rest of the dancers change outfit, we're left with an empty stage. The silence is filled by obscene catcalls from the audience.

This is how the rest of the night goes. The three of us spend the night howling with laughter, not because we're enjoying the show, but because it's so bad it's the only thing we can do.

To the delight of the shrieking audience the next guy comes on stage naked, he needn't have bothered for me. He's scrawny with no muscle definition at all, and greasy, fake black hair that's held back in a ponytail. His cock seems abnormally long and skinny. That can't be natural. It looks likes he's been hanging a rock from the end to lengthen it. I'm sure I've read of jungle tribes who do that. His performance consists of nothing more than him emptying a whole bottle of baby lotion on his appendage and swinging his manhood in a circle so the lotion flies off into the audience. I'm sat there open mouthed at how un-erotic the whole thing is, but from the volume of screaming and obscene offers from the front row of the stalls, I'm obviously in the minority.

At least I know what I *don't* want from the strippers in my book.

The music had been uninspiring and mostly unsuited to the performances. I'd spent ages trawling YouTube for suitable music for my book playlist, playing tracks on repeat until I had the routines perfect in my mind and the timing of the moves down pat. I'd really enjoyed discovering new bands and had a definite rock theme going with the book. I'd chosen Warrant, Nickelback, Hinder, and Three Doors Down to accompany my dancers.

I can't listen to a decent rock track now without choreographing a strip routine in my head at the same time.

I leave the theatre disappointed with the show, but brimming with ideas for my new book. I want my strippers to tell a story with their routines. I want them to have rhythm and to work together well. I think the best examples I've come across in my research so far are videos of an Australian group called 'Thunder Down Under'. Not only do they dance well, but they look great. They're how I picture my characters.

I think back to the girls in the pub at the start of the evening. That whole episode makes me want to create a character who has a quickie in a toilet stall, then is disappointed by the strippers sexual performance. It will serve her right for objectifying him. I want a lead character that wants to be more than a traditional stripper, who fell into stripping by accident. I want a heroine who's not interested in strippers, if anything they're her antithesis. I want a stripper who's the opposite of the hero, a male whore who is just in it for the women. I've so many ideas filling my head right now; I know I'm not going to be able to sleep.

I settle down at my laptop and let my characters tell me their story.

Chapter Six The Gym

I'm a great believer in coincidence and fate. No sooner have I amended my gym membership, because let's face it, I've been paying every month and not going, than the phone rings and it's a personal trainer from the gym.

I'd rung up to try and cancel the monthly fee, but had been persuaded to leave it on a rolling month contract. I know! I've rung to cancel and been talked into staying, but at least I can get out of it with a months notice and truth be told, my ass and belly are in serious need of some attention right now, not to mention how unfit I am. I think the incident with the bicycle has proved that.

The young man on the end of the phone persuaded me to come in and try a personal training session with him and as I was brought up to be polite I felt duty bound to book a session for later this week. I'm a realist. No one is ever going to invent a magic pill to lift a sagging ass, or deflate a podgy belly. With this in mind I'd had to admit to myself that it was time I took an active part in trying to reverse the abuse I'd put my body through.

Whilst being an erotic author sounds like a pretty cool way to earn a living, and most of the time it is, it's also a very sedentary occupation. I spend most of my day sitting at a laptop or curled up in the comforting embrace of my sofa with my iPad. If I'm brutally honest I've pretty much turned into a hermit as well, I can go a whole week without seeing another person aside from the lady in the shop when I go buy my chocolate biscuits.

Age may create a fine wine, but it sure as hell doesn't create a fine body. I'm not sure that mine was ever taut and perfect, but I do recall once having a flat stomach.. Without the support of my extortionately expensive bra my FF breasts droop closer to my belly every day. I think it's safe to say they'd have less distance to travel to my navel than my neck of late.

I try and recall the gym from the last time I was there. I don't go to an expensive or uber posh gym, I don't even go to a cheap and cheerful gym. I just go to a cheap gym. When was the last time you walked into a gym and saw anyone looking cheerful, aside from the look of relief on faces as they leave the premises?

My gym is set over two floors. There are separate men and women's communal changing rooms at the back and side of the ground floor, a large open area full of weights and weight machines in front of the reception and the end of the building is filled with several rows of aerobic machines like treadmills and cross trainers all facing a large and very unflattering mirror.

Upstairs is a room filled with more aerobic and weight equipment, a large alcove with a boxing bag, some mats and exercise balls and the fitness studio. The only reason I even know the upstairs exists is because my sports physio is up there.

From the moment I walk in the door and am faced with the weight lifting regulars to the moment I exit I feel out of place. I'm no gym bunny; I hate exercise for a start and am much happier to be found plodding along the street doing my interpretation of running. I only joined the gym to have somewhere to train for a marathon when the weather was bad. I think that means that I've been twice since I took out my membership almost a year ago. That doesn't mean the weather has been good, it just means the plans for the marathon went out the window!

As I sit here chewing on the end of my cheap pen, hoping I don't have blue ink all over my face again, I try and imagine any way in which the gym could give me inspiration for an erotic scene.

Nothing is coming to mind. I think I'll just go grab a coffee and a chocolate digestive and see if that fuels the imagination.

I picture the gym in my mind. Where could I write a hot scene? Ideally I'd like to set it somewhere that's unique to the gym. As tempting as bending over the desk in the office sounds, I could do that anywhere. The same goes for the showers in the changing rooms.

I'm looking for a piece of equipment I guess that won't require either of us to be a contortionist, or leave me battered and bruised. That's the rowing machine and cross trainer ruled out. What about the treadmill? Whilst the support bars would give me something to hold onto I'm pretty sure that in the throes of passion I'd forget to keep moving my legs and end up travelling off the end and landing in an undignified heap on the floor. Damn. That's another one out.

Of course it would help if I were more intimately acquainted with the gym. It's that long since my last visit I can barely remember what equipment they have in there. It's time to use my favorite research tool – Google!

For some reason the images of weight benches remind me too much of a dentist chair. Yes, they look lovely and supportive for my back, but they don't make me go ooh! The cable machines don't do it for me either. I have visions of getting caught up in the cables somehow, although some of those wrist straps do raise a small tingle in my lady parts at the thought of a bondage element.

My attention is caught by a sit up bench.

It looks so innocent. It's raised at one end with a bar for you to hook your feet under, and as it reclines back down to the floor it offers you cushioning for your back. I think I could do something with this.

If I hook my legs over the bar at the top and lean back…

The door to the gym creaks open, the hinges need some oil. I look around me, hoping they haven't alerted my trainer to my presence yet. Phil stays late for me on a Thursday after normal gym closing hours, meaning it's just him and me. There's no one else to witness my embarrassment.

I used to be a large girl, and in my head I still haven't lost that weight. When I look in a mirror it's the larger me that stares back. My friends constantly tell me that I look fine, but it's going to take some getting used to.

The downside of losing so much weight is the saggy belly that has been left behind. I'm quite clever with my outfit choices, they hide it well and I tend to showcase my best feature – my legs.

I've yet to find a gym outfit that hides anything, especially my blushes. Do clothing manufacturers think that only size six models attend the gym? They seriously need to rethink their marketing approach. Even with all the weight that I have lost I still find myself having to buy a size XL in gym tops. Let's not even mention the re-enforced sports bra that has straps so wide you could walk across them.

I'm wearing all black tonight; it's the most slimming color that I've found. It's also the most forgiving.

I hide in the shadows, watching Phil finish off his own workout. He's taken his shirt off and the sweat glistens and runs down his toned and tattooed back. He's got a tattoo of death that covers the whole of his back and I'm tempted to trail my fingers down it. The artwork calls to me, tempting me, demanding I move closer to inspect it.

Thankfully the lighting in the gym is dimmed with everyone gone, the only light in the alcove where Phil is working out. I hug the shadows of the wall as I move slowly closer.

Phil lowers the weight to the ground, his movements slow and controlled. He moves into his stretches, his flexibility making my mouth water. I wonder what it would be like to make love with someone as flexible as he is. Who am I kidding? It wouldn't be making love with him; it would be pure, animalistic fucking. Just the thought of it makes me wet.

I'm not as stealthy as I had hoped and I catch one of the hand weights with my foot. It makes a metallic clang that seems to echo through the room. Shit.

Phil looks over to where I'm standing, an embarrassed blush crossing my face. He's got to know that I was watching him.

'Hey, Alice. You're early.' He comments. 'You want to go and do a warm up on the treadmill whilst I finish off my stretches?' I nod in agreement, the words failing to materialize from my mouth.

There's a treadmill fairly close to the weights area and I choose that one. I set the warm up routine for five minutes as I've been trained to and start moving. The playlist offers me some gentle rock music for my warm up, I don't want to overdo it, just loosen myself up a little for whatever routine Phil has worked out for me tonight.

I'm lost in the music and am startled by Phil's appearance at my side, almost losing my footing till he puts out a steadying arm. There's a buzz on my skin where he touches me. It's like a gentle jolt of electricity. I briefly turn my head to him and can see that he felt it too. I didn't imagine the spark between us.

There's no way that Phil could find me attractive, I don't even find myself attractive so I can't see how any one else could. It's just my over fertile imagination tormenting me.

The treadmill reduces in speed at the end of the workout and I slow my steps accordingly. Once again Phil reaches over for my arm, guiding me from the machine. I can feel the heat between us. Who am I kidding, that's just the heat from our workouts.

Next he guides me through a series of stretches and moves designed to keep me flexible and warmed up. I feel out of place swinging my arms wide and around, more suited to a cage in a zoo than a gym.

'That was great, Alice. You're getting much better at this.' Phil praises me. That bloody heat returns to my face at his words. One day I'll be able to accept a compliment; I'm just not there yet. 'Let's move over and do some sit ups.' Phil guides me over to the sit up bench, again touching my arm lightly as we move. I sneak a glance at his hand on my bicep; he never touches me normally unless it's to correct a position I'm stretching in. This is new, and not entirely unwelcome, although it does leave me feeling slightly uncomfortable. It's not his touch that's unwelcome; it's the sexual frustration I'm beginning to feel knowing that this won't go any further.

The sit up bench cushions my back as I lie down and hook my ankles under the bars at the top. The blood rushes down to my head and I need a moment to pull myself together.

'Right, Alice, I think we can manage twenty sit ups tonight don't you?' He smirks at me. Normally he only increases the set by a couple each session, tonight he's asking me to add another six from last time.

I groan, audibly. I hate and detest sit-ups. They're hard work, but a necessary evil if I want to lose this jelly belly. Phil just laughs at me and gives me that knowing look. He might believe I can do it, I'm not so sure.

Phil watches me from the side as I struggle through the first few.   He's talking to me quietly, gently encouraging me.

'Let me move down here.' He suggests, moving to stand in front of my feet and allowing him a view straight down my body. 'Now that's a much better view.' He grins.

I realize that my top has ridden up on my body, showing off what looks to be a very toned flat stomach. It's got to be the angle, as it sure as hell doesn't look like that in the mirror!

I maintain my slow but steady pace and concentrate on raising my shoulders, rather than my head. I tune Phil out, focusing just on the count in my head.

'Thank God.' I exhale as I complete the fifteenth sit up, crashing out of breath back onto the comfort of the backrest. 'I'm fucked!'

'Not yet you're not.' Phil laughs. There's something different in his tone, and I raise my weary head to look up at him. Holy shit. He's sporting a hard on in those tiny shorts of his. I'm not sure where to look, but I can't seem to look away.

He's looking at me as though he wants to devour me. I'm getting more frustrated and more worked up here.

Phil reaches down and unhooks my feet from the supports, but instead of letting go of my legs he pulls me up the bench, stopping only when my ass is at the top and my legs are hanging over the end. My pussy is level with his cock at this angle and the thoughts that are currently running through my mind are anything but pure or gym like.

'What?' I manage to croak out.

'Shh.' Phil soothes and leans over to trace his fingers between my legs. Fuck! That feels amazing even through the two layers of thin fabric. With his other hand he massages his erect cock through the material of his shorts. 'I think you're ready for a different, more enjoyable kind of workout.'

'What?' Shit, I really need to get a grip on my vocabulary here. It's beyond basic.

'Just lean back and enjoy.' Phil instructs me as he pulls my Capri leggings and pants off my legs. Now his fingers are tracing my naked flesh and I *want to jump at the sensation. It feels so bloody good.*

His slow, gentle teasing stops suddenly as he thrusts a finger into me.

'Fuck, you're wet Alice.' He grins. He's right. I can feel it. He fucks me with his finger as his thumb massages my clit, and before I know it my back is arching from the bench in a mind-blowing orgasm.

'That was amazing.' I whisper, awe struck.

'That was nothing.' Phil replies. Before I realize what's happening he's removed his finger and replaced it with his cock. He pushes in and then pauses, allowing me a moment to adjust to him. He's certainly well endowed. I can feel the pressure of him filling me. It feels amazing. Again my grammar has abandoned me. Surely I should be able to think of a better word, a word I haven't already used. I can't think though as his cock starts to thrust slowly in and out. He's teasing me. His

cock moving in deep, then drawing back almost to the point of withdrawal. He laughs at my groan as he pulls back.

'Patience, Alice. Patience.'

His movements get deeper and faster, each time he withdraws a little less. I can feel his cock moving against my pussy walls and I'm lost for words. I can however moan in appreciation, loudly.

'That's it Alice, let me know you're enjoying it.' He encourages me. His movements are harder now. At this angle I can feel his balls slapping against my naked flesh. Each time he goes deeper I think that must be it, and each time he surprises me. I've never had sex like this before. I am being well and truly fucked here.

I think he's just about to come, but he slows down instead, swiveling his hips in a circular motion and my back arches from the bench again. Holy Hell! I wondered what it would be like fucking someone flexible like Phil and it's better than anything I imagined.

Each time I think he's about to come, he repeats this, slowing down and rotating his hips. Christ he's got some stamina.

Phil's eyes are lowered, he's watching where our bodies are joined, mesmerized by the push and pull of his cock in me. I'm at the wrong angle to see it, it must be an amazing sight, but for now all I can do is lie back and enjoy the sensations flooding through my body.

I raise my hips to pull him deeper into me each time he thrusts, but I can feel the sweat running down my back, trying to hold me to the bench. I've lost track of time here, I've never had a lover who could last this long, nor one who made me feel as full as Phil does.

Phil starts to move faster and deeper again. I can't stop myself from crying out 'Harder.' He doesn't disappoint me. His cock rams into me so hard I can feel myself being pushed back down the bench, yet Phil has a tight grasp of my hips, pulling me back. His fingers digging in so deeply I'm sure there'll be bruises in the morning. His moans become louder as do mine, I'm almost climaxing again. With a loud bellow he comes inside me, pushing me over the edge and fireworks explode behind my closed eyes.

It takes me a few minutes to come back down to reality. Phil is still standing there at the end of the bench, still slowly moving in and out of me, sweat pouring down his chiseled abs and with a huge shit eating grin on his face.

'That was…' I can't find the words again. Phil just nods his head at me.

'I know. It was.'

'That was the best sex I've ever had.' I finally croak out.

I look at the words I've typed on the screen and cross my legs, trying to ease the ache between them. Now that's a fantasy worthy of the gym.

Sadly, I think the reality is going to be a hell of a lot different to that.

The gym door doesn't creak as I open it; it's well oiled and leads me into an overly bright room full of equipment and people. It's all so familiar, and yet there's nothing to endear me to it. I just want to go home.

The girl behind the reception desk is toned, young and thin. I hate her already.

'How can I help you today?' She greets me in that saccharine sweet voice that grates on my nerves. Did I mention she's blonde and has perky but small artificial tits. Mine may be saggy and past it but at least they're real.

'I've got a training session booked.' I offer, my voice devoid of emotion.

'What's your name please?' She questions.

'Alice.' I respond quietly, almost as if I'm afraid I'll be overheard.

'And who's your appointment with?' She continues.

I look at her blankly, for the life of me I can't remember and grudgingly admit it.

'That's fine, I'll just check the diary for you.' She looks down at the paper diary, I'd have thought it would all have been computerized these days but perhaps that's above her skillset I think, my inner bitch rising to the surface. 'Ah yes. You're booked in with Dom.' She smiles.

Dom? Now that conjures up some erotic images in my head I can tell you, and they involve paddles and spankings and handcuffs. I almost smile until I see the man in question walking over to us, summoned by the Barbie lookalike receptionist.

He's young; in fact he's so young he doesn't look old enough to have left school yet. He's lean, not the toned and chiseled training instructor of my fantasies. Disappointed would be an understatement.

I follow Dom lamely to the office and go through the routine questions and diet checks before heading back out to the gym proper. Once we've got the warm up and stretches out of the way he proceeds to put me through the most humiliating workout I've ever experienced. My only consolation is that we're on the upper floor out of sight of almost everyone.

I'm given stretches that leave my ass in the air and my head between my knees, sit ups against the plastic wall of the mezzanine and various bits of equipment to move with that wouldn't be out of place in a torture chamber.

In short there is nothing erotic or even remotely enjoyable about the whole hour session. I leave the floor a sweaty hot mess and almost lose my footing going down the stairs. This is not how it was supposed to be.

Stripping off my gym gear I head into the shower, the only good thing about the whole day. I let the warm jet of water caress my sensitive skin, hoping it will massage the aches away from my back and shoulders. I'm pretty sure I'm going to need to book a physio session to get over this.

Dressing in my comfortable uniform of jeans and a t-shirt I try to leave the gym unnoticed, fearful that Dom will find me and ask if I'd look to book a series of these torture sessions. No way in hell!

I spent the afternoon recovering on the sofa with my Kindle and a packet of plain chocolate digestives. I also consumed copious amounts of coffee. This was the routine I was used to and comfortable with.

I was so engrossed in the new book that I was reading, and telling myself just one more chapter, that it was three am before I put my Kindle down. It had been worth it. I'd thoroughly enjoyed the book, which was devoid of any mention of gyms or exercise, but did include a healthy dose of hot sex.

Setting my Kindle aside on the coffee table I attempted to rise from the sofa and found out first hand why I am not a candidate for a personal trainer at the gym. Pain shot through my legs and I practically had to crawl to the bathroom and then my bed.

Alice, I promised, I hereby absolve you of all exercise other than hot sex going forward. I thought that was a pretty good bargain with myself.

Chapter Seven — The Journey To Edinburgh

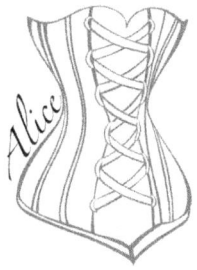

The problem with reading until three am becomes apparent when you have to be at the station for nine am. I have a three-hour train journey ahead of me. Common sense dictates that I should have finished that book on the train rather than reading through the night, but when have I ever done the sensible thing?

The gym session has finished off my back. I am definitely going to book a massage when I get back from the weekend. I'm walking like an old woman, and everything hurts. Parts I never knew existed are protesting. Thankfully, I booked first class. I'm hoping to spend some time writing my stripper book on the train journey to Edinburgh.

I'm attending my first ever book signing. I didn't know these things existed a year ago, and now I'm actually going to meet some of my favorite Australian authors. I'm beyond excited.

I guess I should be nervous about attending on my own, but everyone in the Facebook group has made me feel so welcome, and I'm meeting up with one of the bloggers I know, Chantelle. We've never met, but have become great friends on Facebook. I'm hoping we get on as, thanks to a mix up with her hotel booking, we're sharing a bed tonight!

Chantelle is writing her first book and it's about two women having an intimate relationship. She joked about us doing research in the shower. I countered with research for my next biker book, which would involve finding new ways of killing a character. We agreed there'd be no research this weekend.

One of the authors I'm going to meet, Tina Gephart, wrote a character that really influenced me. Lexi is such a strong personality; no matter what she endured, she got up, brushed herself off, and carried on. She's also a fascinating character, I'm intrigued by the fact she can put a condom on a cock using only her mouth. Now that's a skill I'd like to master one day!

Lexi seemed so real and genuine. Reading these books got me through some very dark days. Seeing a woman that overcame so much in the book made me question why I was living a life I was so miserable with. I wanted to be more like Lexi. I came across her in the first book, 'A Twist of Fate', and have since devoured the rest of the series. I can't believe I'm getting to meet her creator today.

The train journey passes without incident, and seems to go so quickly. Looking at the half chapter

I've managed to write I wonder where the time went. I suspect a large part of it was shuffling in my seat, trying to get comfortable.

The gym session from yesterday comes back to haunt me as I try and get off the train. Every muscle has tightened up. Thankfully this station is the terminus, so there's no rush. The downside of travelling first class is that my carriage is at the furthest end of the train. My hips and calves are demonstrating their displeasure at being asked to perform any movement.

I've been to Edinburgh a few times, but I'm not familiar with the area where my accommodation is. I take the cheats way out and flag down a taxi.

The accommodation is a student property; as it's out of term time they rent it out. It's clean, its basic and I'm delighted to see there are plenty of plug sockets to charge my phone and iPad, as well as plug in my straighteners and hair dryer. That's when I notice that there isn't a mirror anywhere near a socket. Have you ever used an iPad as a mirror? It's like the hall of mirrors at the fun fair – it makes you look twice the size and is unflattering as hell.

The double bed is on the small side and flush to the wall. There's just enough space for my suitcase and handbag. That said the room has everything I need and was a fraction of the cost of some of the other accommodation.

I decide to walk into Edinburgh as I have enough time before I'm due to meet up with Tina. She agreed to meet up with me after the authors lunch this afternoon. The walk will do me good.

Famous. Last. Words. Did you know Edinburgh has hills? It has lots of them. And they're all uphill from the room I'm staying in. I follow Google Maps for about fifteen minutes before I realize the map is upside down. My legs are far from impressed. Surely Google Maps should show the map the same way up as the phone. Pfft.

The closer I get to the pub we've agreed to meet at, the more excited I am. I'm actually going to meet a real life author. One whose books I devour and adore. I would pinch myself if every part of me weren't already hurting.

When I arrive at the pub I find out the author lunch is running late. I scan the other customers, trying to work out who else could be here for the signing. The problem with book readers is they look just like you and me. Still, as I sit there with my cup of black coffee, mourning the lack of a chocolate digestive biscuit, I enjoy a session of people watching.

According to Facebook several other readers have arrived in Edinburgh, and one kind soul takes pity on me and offers to come join me. There's this great thing about the people on the Facebook group, they make you feel like one of them. Pretty soon the booth I'm sitting in is full of other readers, all excited for the signing tomorrow, all sharing a common interest. It didn't feel like a table of strangers, it felt like a meeting of old friends.

It wasn't long before the author lunch was over and there she was. This amazing, talented, and wonderful lady was chatting to me! Again, it felt like meeting up with an old friend that you hadn't seen for years, instead of someone for the first time. My day had been made.

I've only done karaoke a couple of times in my life, and both of them had involved copious amounts of alcohol first. Not this evening. The atmosphere at the evening event was such that I got sucked in. Chantelle had joined me, but we'd become split up almost instantly after buying our drinks. Seating was at a premium so I found a spare chair practically at the side of the stage and laid claim to it. Again, fellow readers made me feel so welcome. The bonus for me was the proximity to Tina and a few of my other favorite Australian authors. Being this close to them felt surreal. Even though I had a couple of books under my belt by this point, I didn't feel like an author. I felt like a fan girl.

By the time I'd plucked up the courage to have a go at the Karaoke, and found a willing co-conspirator, most of the songs I knew had gone. We agreed we'd do a Tina Turner song, the one about wheels turning. Trying to climb up on the stage in my tight leather skirt and with barely any movement in my back proved interesting, but not as interesting as being presented with an alternative version of the song we were supposed to sing. It had a totally different pace to the original. Luckily for me everyone had had so much to drink by this point that no one noticed how genuinely tuneless I was.

Catching up with Chantelle again we decided to head back to the hotel, a long day ahead of us in the morning. Have you ever been in a taxi in Edinburgh? They're like the black cabs in London. They have a stupidly high step to get into them, and you need to duck your head. Neither of which was conducive to the current state of my body. I'm not sure if the poor taxi driver thought I was drunk or on drugs, such was the performance I made trying to get in. Finally, after smacking my head on the roof of the doorframe, I succeeded.

Thankfully Chantelle and I had the best nights sleep in our tiny double bed, and no book research was carried out.

Chapter Eight – The Book Signing

If anyone ever tells you to get a wheeled bag to carry all your books at a book signing, ignore them. Or invest in a heavy-duty version. Before we'd got to the front door of the signing venue one of the wheels had fallen off my trolley. It only had six books in it!

In hindsight a heavy-duty granny shopping trolley would have been better. Hindsight is a wonderful thing.

Chantelle and I split up once we got inside, both of us having different lists of authors we wanted to meet. Half dragging my trolley behind me, having to stoop, as it was now too short for my 5'7' height, coupled with day two post gym muscle fatigue that is much worse than day one, I must have presented an interesting sight. I probably also resembled a small child in a sweet shop.

The large, bright room was filled with tables full of authors and books. I was in reader heaven. I was also nervous as hell. I'd never done this before. Let's just say, I almost wet my pants when I realized that a whole group of my favorite authors were side by side in one aisle.

I'm not sure I can do justice to how amazing a book signing is. The camaraderie of fellow readers was amazing, as was meeting up with some people I had so far only known through Facebook. But meeting the authors! It was like meeting royalty. You know what though? Authors are just normal people like you and me. They get nervous at book signings as well, and they love meeting readers, old and new alike.

The atmosphere was electric throughout. I don't know what I'd expected, but it wasn't the reality, that was so much better. I chatted to authors whose books I had read and loved. There were authors from around the world and they'd gathered together in this one room for us. It made me more determined to go ahead in organizing a book signing in my hometown. I wanted to share this experience.

About an hour before the signing ended my trolley gave up the ghost, the second wheel fell off as well. Now I really was bent in half trying to drag the trolley around. Despite only taking a few books I was getting signed for a friend, I was going home with way more than I could carry.

The reality of just how many books I had became apparent when we got back to our accommodation. There was no way the books would fit in the suitcase I'd brought, even without my clothes or toiletries going in there. A trip to Primark was needed.

If you ever go to a book signing I suggest you wear the most comfortable footwear you can find. I wish I'd had a pedometer to tell me how many miles I walked. I'm pretty sure it was a high number. The reality of just how much mileage you do became apparent when we bumped into a fellow attendee in the lift at Primark who was proudly sporting a pair of new, fluffy, and very comfortable slippers. She'd given up on her shoes and come and bought the slippers for the evening event. As I looked at the shiny, black suitcase that I'd just purchased, I confess I was regretting not buying the slippers myself.

My first book signing was an amazing experience, and one that I dreamed of undertaking as an author one day, even if I had to organize it myself.

Chapter Nine - The Massage

After my non-adventure at the gym and my weekend in Edinburgh, I feel like a bloody old woman.

There's nothing else for it. I'm going to have to book a massage. Massage sounds so sensual doesn't it, but I see a sports physio. That means there's a lot of moaning and groaning like you get in sex, but without the pleasure. It's a good job there isn't a swear jar in the room some days, as I'd be bankrupt otherwise. That said if I'm swearing, then I know he's doing a decent job of it.

I'm not old per-se, but I am rather past it. My left hip is buggered, my right ankle is delicate, my knees are screwed, and I stuffed something up in my right shoulder moving house. Let's just say if I were a horse they'd have taken me outside and put me out of my misery by now. The physio at the hospital came out with some fancy phrase about my biomechanics being out of alignment. That's about all she did though, aside from setting me some simple exercises. Do I look like I want exercises? No. I want a hands on approach. Preferably some tall, dark and handsome therapist who will soothe away my aches and pains with his healing hands.

Will I get a hands on approach? Will I hell. The way my luck goes I'll be lucky to get any type of approach these days.

That doesn't stop me daydreaming though. What would it be like if my imagination wrote the scene. I think this calls for coffee, chocolate digestives, and a session on the MacBook!

The waiting room is sumptuous with long black leather sofas that you can sink into, and I do. Bliss. That said I'm not sure how I am going to get my ass off here gracefully when it's time for my appointment. I'm not graceful on a good day and today is definitely not one of those. My back and shoulders are killing me, but what can I expect after a rather hot sex session in the gym. It was worth every ache and I'd do it all again at the drop of a hat if it was offered.

There's soft rock music playing over the intercom, none of that muzak crap you often hear in lifts. It's more ballad than anything and it's very soothing. The receptionist offered me a drink, as I was early for my appointment, and to my utter joy it was none of that healthy crap, it was a caramel macchiato latte. I'm ensconced on this luxurious sofa with my latte and my Kindle, and for a moment I almost forget why I am here. The nagging pain at the base of my neck seems to have eased off momentarily as my senses are distracted by the comfort of my surroundings.

I'm not even bothered by the friendly receptionist with her long blonde hair that looks like she has it professionally styled, or her perfectly manicured Barbie pink nails. I'm actually slightly jealous of her nails. I look at the stumps of what's left of mine and draw in a sad breath, mourning the loss of my beloved talons in a cleaning accident. Who'd have thought being house-proud could be so detrimental to your appearance. Come to think of it, perhaps it wouldn't have hurt to put the straighteners through my hair rather than just throwing it back in a barely brushed messy ponytail this morning. It's too late now though. Besides, she's at least twenty years younger than me and I'm sure there's some unspoken rule that says women over a certain age don't have to bother as much anymore. Who am I kidding? The fact that I don't bother at all is probably why I rely so much on my imagination for any adventure in my life.

Her slim fitting skirt shows no trace of belly, whereas my jeans sit just below mine, highlighting yet another part of me that has sagged as I've got older. I've always wanted to rock that hot sexy secretary look; I've never achieved it though. I kind of rock a grunge look these days.

The door opens and the noise of the street interrupts my tranquil moment. A woman much older than me walks in. She's gone for the brash look, and pretty much everything about her is artificial from her overly pert breasts to her plumped up lips. She looks over in my direction, her curiosity giving way to a look of disdain when she catches sight of my less than perfect appearance. Hey! I may not be perfect, but at least I'm not plastic. She's had so many nips and tucks I suspect that her ass is probably sat right under her nose judging from the way she looks as though she just smelled something bad.

'Is Carlo available today?' she asks the receptionist, her voice oozing money and expectation. The girl looks over at me apologetically before advising her that he's already booked this morning.

'I could book you in with Marian though, she's free,' she offers instead. The snooty customer looks even more put out at that thought.

'No, no. That won't do at all,' she mutters. 'I need Carlo's special brand of attention. Marian just won't do. It simply won't do.' She throws me an even filthier look than before. 'Unless, of course, you wouldn't mind swapping with me?' She questions, throwing a fake grin in my direction.

Now normally I'm a pretty easy-going person and would have swapped. It's really no skin off my nose whether it's Carlo or Marian who sees to me just as long as they undo the bloody damage I've inflicted on myself. However, this particular woman has my shackles raised. The snooty cow looked at me like I was something she'd brought in on the bottom of her shoe when she first arrived and now she thinks I'm going to swap masseurs with her.

'I'm so sorry,' I smile sweetly. 'I'm in need of Carlo's particular attention myself this morning, I'm afraid.' She looks horrified at the thought of Carlo wanting to pay attention to anyone but her, and that just makes me smile more. 'Up yours bitch,' I mentally high five myself.

There's no sound to indicate the door at the end of the waiting room has opened, but something draws her attention. She moves away from the receptionist, now ignored, and throws her arms wide towards whoever has just entered the room. I look over and my jaw drops, literally. Standing before me is a tall, hot hunk. Please tell me this is Carlo. My mouth starts to water at the same time my lady parts do. Holy Hell. He's got tanned olive skin, dark hair, and even darker eyes.

'Carlo, darling. There's been some terrible mistake. I need you to take care of me now,' she pouts. Pass me a sick bag. This performance is vomit inducing.

Carlo looks startled for a moment and turns to the receptionist for assistance. 'I didn't think Mrs Thwaite was booked in today?' he queries. Is that a tremor I can hear in his voice? Nah, can't be. I'm just imagining it. Then again she is a pretty scary sight.

'She isn't. Your client, Alice, is over there.' The receptionist just went up in my estimation by pointing at me. This is Carlo? If I'd known he looked like this I'd have booked in for a massage every day this week!

Carlo makes the appropriate soothing noises to Mrs Snooty Bitch who is obviously not impressed. She turns and huffs her way out of the door. He lets out a deep sigh before looking back to reception. 'If she comes back, tell her I went home sick,' he whispered. The receptionist just laughs, obviously privy to some inside joke.

Carlo moves over to where I'm sitting and offers me his hand. 'You must be Alice, pleasure to meet you.'

There's a hint of an accent in his voice that I can't quite place. There's a touch of drawl. It's hot as hell. I'd be quite happy to just sit here, watch and listen to him talk all day.

'Shall we?' He indicates the open door. Oh yes please!

The lighting in the treatment room is muted and the same music is playing in here as in reception. There's a scented candle lit in one corner, but it's not the sickly sweet aroma you get from some. There's a hint of musk there I'm sure. Again, like the reception area, the mood in here is soft and sensual.

I'd expected a standard looking clinical massage table, but what's in front of me looks more like a single bed in size. It's raised from the floor and covered in crisp, yet soft, white cotton. I trace my fingers along it wondering just how high this thread count is and realizing it's probably way out of my budget.

Carlo shows me where to get changed, behind an intricate looking Chinese screen. There's even a proper hanger for my clothes. This is so different to my normal experience where I quickly change in the gym changing room before rushing up stairs to the treatment room in my shorts and vest.

I've just stripped down to my bra and knickers when I hear Carlo advise me that I should remove everything and wrap myself in a towel. Even the towels are soft and fluffy in this place. They're so white they look like they're brand new, and they're thick and luxurious against my skin. Despite how comfortable the towel is I'm a little disconcerted at the thought of my nakedness beneath it. I don't even get naked at home unless all the lights are off.

When I come out from behind the screen Carlo has lowered the lights even more. The room is dim, and in this light even my fat ass will look good. I exhale a sigh of relief.

I'm expecting to be asked a barrage of questions before we begin, but there's nothing. Instead Carlo indicates the bed between us. I lay down as carefully as I can without disturbing the towel to realize that I've got it fastened tightly between my breasts and need to loosen it off so it can be lowered. Once that embarrassment is over with, I tremble with shock at the feel of his fingers on my lower back. My body sinks into the mattress that's more comfortable than my bed at home.

'Shh,' he soothes. 'Just lay there and relax.' His fingers gently caress all of my back, slowly and far too sensually for a massage. It feels amazing *though, especially when he traces his fingers in light lazy circles around the base of my spine.*

He takes his hands away for a moment and I almost cry out in desperation, but it's only to warm some massage oil in his palms. The oil feels warm on my skin and very luxurious. This is more like a pamper session than a massage. The oil must have something in it because I can feel my back heating up, just enough to be comfortable. There's a faint hint of spice in the air, which I think might be cinnamon. Whatever it is, it's pleasant.

Carlo strokes his hands sensually up and down my back, applying just a little more pressure with each pass. Each time, the towel seems to move just a little lower than the one before. His firm hands cup the swell of my ass on the next stroke. I'm not sure whether I should be offended here, but it feels so damned good I choose to keep my mouth shut. I don't want him to stop that's for sure.

There's a subtle movement and then I feel Carlo on the bed with me. It's just wide enough for him to be able to place his knees either side of my legs. He hovers there, just above my ass as he continues the firm but relaxing massage along my spine.

I'm embarrassed to say that the whole thing is getting me wet. Right now I have some very impure and improper thoughts buzzing around my head.

Carlo leans closer to me as he applies more pressure around my neck and shoulders. His hands almost closing around my throat each time, his head so close to mine now that I can feel his breath against my ear.

Holy shit! That can't be right! I almost rise up in protest as I feel his hard abs pressing against my spine, but it's the hard length between his legs pushing against my ass that has me so shocked. He's bloody naked!

Now, if this was one of my novels that would be fine, but it isn't. Part of me is yelling to get the fuck out of here now, but the other part is saying stay the hell where I am and see where this goes. Of course, being the author that I am, I decide to stick it out. I justify it by telling myself I can use it for book research.

Carlo's body seems to mold perfectly against mine. The gentle sweep of his hands seems to only make me wetter with each pass over my back. He's softly whispering in my ear in some foreign language. I have no idea what the hell he's saying, but it sounds hot so I just go with it. For all I know he could be reciting his grandmothers shopping list.

His hard cock keeps pushing up against my saggy ass and it feels huge. At least it appears pleased to see me judging by how often it's nudging me. His hands move lower down my spine, kneading my ass in small circles when I'm suddenly surprised by a slap. It shocks the hell out of me. I haven't been slapped on the ass since I was a child and that was by my mother. Back then it was something you'd run away to avoid. It stings, but it's not unpleasant. Right now I'm just wishing he'd do it again. He does, on the other cheek this time. Fuck. His hand must be stinging from that one because my ass certainly is. He soothes away the sting with his soft yet strong hands, all the time moving closer to my wetness. Oh my God. I'm mortified that he's going to find out what he's done to me, how my body is reacting. This is so wrong.

What the hell? I think to myself. I'm laid on a bed with a hot naked guy on top of me who's slapping my ass until it stings and I'm worrying about him finding out how wet he's made me? I mentally berate myself. The whole situation is so bloody wrong to start with, but I'm enjoying it far too much to be offended. Now I can see why the snooty woman was so keen to have an appointment with him.

I've just finished telling myself to shut up and enjoy the experience when his fingers slip between my legs and into me. Holy shit. That feels so good I almost cry out. Instead I bite down on my lip. He fucks me with his fingers a few times before withdrawing them suddenly.

'You taste so good, Alice,' he murmurs. What the hell? He's put his fingers in his mouth? I'm sure that should disgust me, but instead it turns me on. 'You're so wet and ready for me,' he whispers.

The words have barely left his mouth before I feel his cock push into me. Did I say holy hell already? That feels so fucking amazing. My legs are trapped together between his, there's no room for me to move, although I do try and push my ass up at him to draw him in deeper. Deeper? Who am I kidding; in this position I don't think he could get any deeper. I feel full of him; his cock fits me perfectly. He's slowly thrusting in and out. Each time it feels as if he's about to pull out and my greedy pussy really doesn't want that. I groan in protest as it feels as though he's about to slip out, but am rewarded by what feels like an even deeper thrust.

I have to say this is now officially one of my favorite ever sex positions and we've only just started. One moment he's pushing slowly into me with his chest tight against my back, the next he's sat up straight and placed a stinging slap on my ass before thrusting so hard I feel like I'm about to split in two. I don't think I can take much more of this, the sensation is amazing. It's as though he can sense my limit and he changes position slightly, or so I think. I'm wrong, he hasn't moved but his hips have taken over and he's using them in a circle motion. I think I've died and gone to heaven, the feeling is out of this world.

The slow twist turns back into gentle thrusts before progressing into the deep hard penetration again. My senses are on overload here. This is definitely the laziest position for sex I've found for me, but it's also the hottest as well. Each time he pushes into me so deeply that I can feel his balls slapping against me. I'm so wet I can feel that as well.

When I think he must be about to come he goes back to the rolling motion with his hips, delaying the inevitable. That movement has me grinning from ear to ear I can tell you.

He's stopped with the slow moves now and is slamming into me again. This is amazing. At this angle he's hitting that magic spot. Just when I think I can't take anymore my orgasm rolls over me. It's as though he was waiting for it. As soon as it hits he lets out a loud roar before coming inside me. Even when he's come he continues to move, slowly.

'That was fucking amazing,' I manage to utter.

'Sure was.' I can hear the smirk in his voice as he collapses down on top of me. It's a strange position to be in. It's not intimate in that I can't see him, but the feel of his chest against my back, that skin on skin contact, and his legs trapping mine between them makes it feel much more intimate than you'd expect.

We stay like that for a few minutes, his cock still hard inside me. This position is so comfortable that I really don't want to move. I do let out a loud groan when he finally moves away from me. I turn onto my side, a smug grin across my face as I watch him towel off the sheen of sweat that coats his body. I'm not surprised, that felt far more strenuous than any workout I've seen at the gym.

That was the best massage – ever! Where do I book in for a repeat!

Writing that chapter has me horny as hell. Somehow I don't think a chocolate digestive and a coffee are going to do it for me. I laugh quietly to myself. That scene is never going to happen in real life. But damn, I wish it would.

My reality is a sweet young guy who tells me all about the holidays he shares with his girlfriend and asks me for advice on buying cars thanks to my past life working in the motor trade. The only heat in that room comes from the fan on the floor, which is there to take the chill off the cold and stark room.

The twinge in my neck and the slight numbness in my fingers tell me it's time to book another appointment with him. One text later and I'm booked in for the following morning.

The problem with my sports physio is that he works out of my gym. So not only do I have the hot memories of the gym scene I wrote as I walk through to the changing room, I also remember the humiliation of the reality.

The changing room is quiet as I place my coat and jeans in the locker. I hate these rooms with their over abundance of mirrors to catch you out and remind you why you need to visit the gym in the first place.

I allow myself a smug grin at the realization that I'm not here to suffer torture today, just the pain of a sports massage. Dressed in a running top and shorts I hurry barefoot through the gym and up the stairs. The door is closed when I get there, but I'm a few minutes early so I sit and wait outside. Careful not to appear a voyeur, I watch the action going on around me and I'm pleased to see I'm not the only one who has to endure humiliating positions at the hands of their personal trainer. That thought quickly brings me back to reality as I look around surreptitiously to make sure my trainer isn't here today. I know he'll ask me when I'm coming back and I'm not sure I can face that again just yet.

The door creaks open and I'm about to utter a cheery hello to Adi, my usual sports physio, when

I'm surprised with the appearance of a brick wall. Okay, that was perhaps a little unkind, but the woman standing before me looks like a bloody Russian shot putter. At least I think it's a woman. She's got one of those close cropped hair styles you see at the Olympics and leaves you guessing the sex until the event name flashes up on screen and lets you know that this is indeed a woman. She's solid that's for sure. She's not cheerful either. Adi is cheerful. Whilst he's pulverizing the hell out of my back and leaving it tender but fixed, he's making me laugh with whatever the latest scrape is that he and his mates got up to since my last visit.

I don't think this woman even knows how to laugh; she looks so serious. She beckons me in with what I think is a grunt, but could have been a greeting, I guess. She advises me that she's covering for Adi today as he's been called to a training day with the local football club that he also works with. I've been stood up for a footballer again. I wouldn't mind so much if I were getting stood up for a hunky rugby player or two, but no. And he's left me with Helga the Horrible as well.

The next half hour is about as far removed from my fantasy as can be. I actually cry real tears at one point. The rest of the time I'm biting my lip to avoid swearing out loud as she digs her meaty fingers into the tight knot at the base of my neck.

She barely utters a sound apart from the odd tut of disgust at the stubbornness of the knot. Instead she works diligently away, inflicting pain on a never felt before scale. Whilst the slaps on my ass were welcome in the fantasy, this pain is the opposite. Each time she digs her fingers in I grimace. This is not an occasion where I want to utter the word deeper or faster, that's for sure.

At the end of the session I can barely move from the table. Whilst the tension in my shoulders has gone, the tenderness in my back makes me cringe every time the light fabric of my t-shirt moves against it. Sleep is going to be almost impossible in this state.

I try and convince myself that it will be fine in the long run, and that by tomorrow this will all have been worth it, but I can't help thinking that I enjoyed my fantasy a hell of a lot more.

If only real life could be as much fun as my imagination.

Chapter Ten At Your Age

Today I'm heading to the doctors office to get a contraceptive implant. I've been using the injection, Depo-provera, for years to control painful periods. When it was first suggested to me, I was advised that one of the potential side effects was that I wouldn't have periods.

'Sign me up now!' I'd demanded. I don't know about you, but that was a major selling point for me.

It worked. For over twelve years I had been happily period free. Then came that last appointment with the nurse. I'd gone along for my regular twelve-week injection wondering if it would be the nice nurse or the butcher. With one I never felt a thing, with the other I had a bruise on my ass for a week.

This particular day, it was the nurse who'd upset me on my previous visit by telling me I was overweight and should weigh the same as I had when I was eighteen. Seriously? I'd refrained from hitting her because she didn't look well.

Today she managed to outdo herself. She advised me I'd need to make an appointment with the doctor to discuss alternative contraceptive methods. Then she used that phrase. 'At your age…'

Apparently at the ripe old age of forty-five I am past it in medical terms. I'm no longer able to enjoy the side effects of Depo-provera because I'm too old to use it anymore. Granted, she did go on to explain that the Depo can contribute to osteoporosis, and that by stopping now I'd have sufficient years left to undo any damage already done. I understood what she was telling me, but did she have to use that particular phrase, 'At your age…'

That phrase has me imagining little old ladies in nursing homes for Gods sake. I'm *not* that old.

So today I'm back at the doctors surgery to have an implant injected into my arm. It was the only option that looked like it may have the same side effect of no periods, and frankly I just didn't like the sound of any of the other alternatives.

The doctor seems cheerful enough and talks me through the procedure. She's going to inject an anesthetic into my arm so I won't feel anything, and then place the implant under the skin on my bicep.

'Before I start, I do need to advise you that it won't be effective as a contraceptive for at least two weeks,' she explains.

I almost fall off the narrow surgery bed from laughing.

'I don't think that will be an issue,' I smile. 'I've just got divorced.'

'No one else on the horizon?' she asks while she waits for the anesthetic to take effect.

'Nope, and not looking.' I've decided that I don't need another man. I certainly don't need another relationship. When I'm ready, if I'm ever ready, I'll just find someone to go out on the odd date with and have hot sex occasionally. No more sharing a house, or life with a man for me. I don't want the white picket fence and happy ever after.

It's that long since I've had sex that I'm pretty sure my vagina has healed up. Let's just say it's been years rather than months.

There's an odd sensation as the implant goes in, but it wasn't painful. If anything it hurt less than getting a Depo injection with the butcher nurse.

I'm still laughing as I head home, remembering the doctor's warning. I can't have unprotected sex for the next two weeks.

Chance would be a fine thing!

Chapter Eleven A Hen Night

On Crack

Before I went to Edinburgh I'd found a local venue to host the book signing I'm organizing next year. Great central location so everyone can get to it regardless of how they travel, whether that's by bus, car or train. We have our own entrance, excellent disabled access, and a large open area outside of the main room where readers can get refreshments and have a break. It's a hotel as well as a conference center so the authors can stay on site. Everything looked to be pretty perfect.

Until yesterday.

Yesterday I got a call from the hotel asking me for more information. Despite top name hotels in Dublin and London hosting book signings it appears that our local hotel is a little cautious about the demographic of my attendees. They don't understand erotic romance at all.

This was the second phone call I received yesterday, the first was worse. That was the local tourist board who politely informed me that they couldn't assist me with promoting my event as they didn't feel it fitted with the image that they wanted to portray of the city. This is a city that is a regular on the hen and stag party calendars. You can't go into the center on a weekend without tripping over a hen or stag and their drunken wedding party.

How could we be worse than that? Did they think we were a hen party on crack or something?

I was insulted.

I was insulted on behalf of the readers. I was insulted on behalf of the authors.

I advised them that actually, I didn't need their help to promote the event; I was more than capable of that. I had simply requested their assistance in getting discounted accommodation deals for my readers and authors. I was trying to bring business to the city. I'd deal with it myself.

What really got to me is that the people making these decisions kept comparing us to 'Fifty Shades of Grey', and hadn't even bothered to read it. They were making an assumption about our readers, without any evidence to back it up.

By now I was furious. The readers I'd come across were friendly, warm, kind hearted, and a bloody good laugh. I'd already promoted the event as suitable for a weekend away with the family. The readers could attend the signing on the Saturday while the family enjoyed the city, and then spend the Sunday together.

Just because the event had a tattooed bad boy theme didn't mean we were going to trash the place. It just meant that as readers we loved to read about bikers, rock stars, and billionaires who have tattoos.

I was almost ready to quit.

I phoned a venue I'd previously discounted, as I thought the signing would be too small for them. They would be happy to accommodate us, and if I wanted, I could come and view the rooms they were suggesting today.

I'm nervously sitting in the administration office waiting area. I'm trying to prepare for the questions about our demographic and erotic books. I needn't have worried.

The room I was shown was stunning. A whole wall of glass looks out over a racecourse. There's an area outside for dealing with tickets and a bar in the room for refreshments. In my minds eye I can picture the sparkle of the glass, with the light bouncing off tables covered in white linen cloths, and the array of bright colors from the book covers. It's going to be stunning.

The organizer offered to email me floor plans that were scaled, so I could work out how much room I have to play with. She then blew me away when she suggested we use a separate floor for our evening event, meaning we wouldn't have to rush to clean up between the day and evening party.

The evening room was equally as stunning, and what's better is that it had two bars. I've seen how some authors drink! There's room for a buffet, a disco and a Photo Booth. It's everything that I wanted and more.

The price is slightly staggering, and I advise her that I'll need to check the figures and get back to her.

When I got home I checked the spreadsheet containing the original budget. It was doable, just.

It was a scary amount of money. What if no one wanted to come? What if authors didn't want to take a chance on an unknown organizer? What if I didn't sell enough tickets to cover the costs? The questions kept coming; one after the other.

I stopped myself. I'd done the math. I knew how many tickets I needed to sell to cover costs. I had to stop listening to that voice in my head that told me I'm not good enough. That was the old Alice. The new Alice wasn't going to listen to that crap anymore.

I picked up the phone and booked the venue. Within minutes the contract was signed and the deposit paid. I was really doing this!

I logged onto my MacBook and started populating the website for the event, then considered the list of authors who'd already expressed an interest if the signing went ahead.

Some of the names on the list had me shaking with excitement. These were my superstars, the authors I admired, and whose books I devoured. I sent the first few invitations, nervous anticipation devouring me.

Within an hour I had half a dozen positive responses and deposits. This was really happening. I couldn't help myself. I started dancing around the living room, squealing with excitement. Oh. My. God.

I was going to meet some of my idols for the first time, not only that, but I'd be signing with them as well.

I couldn't wait for next year. This is what life should be about. Taking chances, believing in yourself, and following your dreams. Bring it on!

Chapter Twelve The Tattoo Shop

I'm looking at my reflection in the mirror and thinking how unforgiving this piece of reflective glass is. When did I get so old? The face looking back at me is weathered and worn, not to mention sporting a bloody scab where I couldn't resist picking a blind zit. Who gets zits over the age of forty, I ask you?

Sighing, I turn away, wondering how I let myself get this way. Granted, I don't follow a skin care regime, but it's not like I'm exposing myself to extreme weather conditions. That said I do love sitting in the garden when the sun is out lost in a book on my Kindle. I may have the occasional session on a sun-bed as well I suppose, but that's only because a tan makes you look slimmer. Well, that's my excuse and I'm sticking to it.

Most of the time I don't feel old. I might look it, but for the first time in ages I probably feel a good ten years younger; once I've woken up properly anyway. I need to do something that will stop me feeling like such an old fart. Ageing may be a natural process, but it's one I plan to embark on artificially and disgracefully.

I turn back to the overly honest mirror, why do hairdressers' mirrors highlight every flaw and imperfection in such detail? It's even given me a double chin! Placing my hand on my soft, protruding belly I guess I should be honest with myself, the double chin is more likely the result of my obsession with dark chocolate biscuits and black coffee.

Dan, my perky young hairdresser moves behind me to inspect the hair dye that's hopefully going to remove all trace of the silver sparkles in my hair, aka my grey roots. These buggers seem to be coming back faster than ever these days; my once bi-monthly appointment is now every four weeks from necessity.

The conversation with the nurse, even though it was months ago, is still on my mind as well. I can't get over her use of the phrase, *'at your age'*. I'm not old! I just feel it.

Needing something more to lift me from this feeling of impending doom and senility, I've taken a drastic step. On the plus side, I'm finally crossing something off my bucket list. On the minus side, I've just signed myself up for several hours of pain. I've booked in for my first tattoo. I've wanted one for years, but could never decide on a design; not to mention spending too much time worrying about what other people would think, rather than concentrating on living the life I wanted. Enough of that mentality. The hair dye is my homage to growing old artificially, the tattoo to doing it disgracefully.

I've taken my time and found the perfect design; it's a tattoo I wrote into one of my books. The center of the design is a detailed skull with roses and leaves threaded through it, circling it is an Oscar Wilde quote – *Every saint has a past, every sinner has a future.* That phrase is perfect for me, representing the life I've left behind and the new future that I am embracing. Because it's in one of my books it also symbolizes me following my dream of becoming a writer.

The fact that my mother has forbidden me from having it done just seems to make it all the more exciting. I'm forty-five, my mother can't still be telling me what I can and can't do, surely? Don't get me wrong, I love her to bits, and truly value her opinion, but this time I'm going to ignore it.

I've booked the appointment for Monday afternoon; it's going to be a long weekend of nerves I suspect. I'm torn between feeling scared and excited. I'm a tough cookie though, I can endure a few hours of pain, and I'm sure the end result will be more than worth it.

Two hours later and I'm sitting in front of my laptop; my freshly colored, styled, and straightened hair is wasted on an unappreciative MacBook. Naturally I'm nibbling away at a plate of Digestives whilst caressing my warm mug of coffee in my other hand. It's time to write. It's not long before my imagination takes me on a journey to the tattoo shop I'm going to be visiting. What will it look like? The only time I've seen the interior of one is on a TV show, LA Ink, and that seemed very clinical and arty.

The shop sits in a small terrace, between a butchers and a post office. The blackened window glass giving no glimpse of what lies within. The sign above the window shows the shop name, intertwined with skulls, roses, and clock faces. The more I stare at it the more hidden gems reveal themselves, a fairy, an angel, and a butterfly so realistic that I'd swear it was mid flight. The exterior looks clean and fresh, no peeling paint or litter, and I find that reassuring.

I pause for a moment admiring the sleek, sporty bike that is parked outside. I know from my Facebook chats with the tattoo artist, Matt, that he's a biker. God, I could imagine some fantasies involving that bike, but right now, I don't have time. The moment has arrived. Confidently, I push the shop door open; it's time to get my virgin skin branded.

The interior of the shop glistens with polished chrome, clinical white tiling, and comfortable looking black leather reclining chairs that transform into something resembling a luxurious massage table.

To my left there's a small reception desk, Matt is sitting there sketching an intricate image of Death. It's so impressive I'm mentally trying to work out where I could have that as a tattoo.

'Hey, Alice. Great to finally meet you.' Matt stands from the desk, coming round it to embrace me in a bear hug.

Wow. I wasn't expecting such an affectionate greeting. Matt is taller than me, has biceps the size of tree trunks, and looks like he works out at the gym. To my utter disappointment he also looks to be twenty years younger than I am. If only I was younger I'd definitely be interested in getting to know him intimately. I need to focus, I'm not sure having fantasies about the guy inking my skin is such a good idea.

'Great to meet you, too.' I mumble. My head is still clasped firmly against his rock hard chest. He smells so good, I've no idea what the fragrance is, but I love it.

Matt guides me to a black leather sofa against the far wall. When we sit I can feel the heat from his thigh pushed against mine. He hands me the design for my tattoo and I can't help the gasp that escapes. It's beautiful. Matt has captured the detail from the original image perfectly. This is going to look amazing.

'You're pleased with it then?' Matt asks.

'I love it!' I really do, it's even better than I imagined.

I should be nervous; it's my first tattoo after all. It's weird, because I've spent so much time chatting with Matt on Facebook he doesn't feel like a stranger; it's more like meeting up with an old friend I haven't seen in ages. I feel totally at ease with him doing my tattoo.

'Great,' Matt grins. 'Let's get started.'

He leads me to one of the chairs and sets it into a reclining position so it looks more like a massage bed. Matt talks me through what he's doing, explaining that he's starting off applying the template to my lower back. Once that is in place, he helps me off the bed and leads me over to a mirror so I can inspect the positioning. It's a lot bigger than I'd originally planned, but he explained it needed to be this size to show off the detail properly. This is definitely growing old disgracefully and I embrace it.

Once I'm back on the bed Matt asks me if I'm ready. I guess this is it. I just hope I can handle the pain I've been warned about by friends. I can do this! I let him know I'm ready and brace myself for the needle.

'Relax, Alice,' Matt soothes, his soft voice as comforting as the gentle caress of his hand on my back. I hear the snap of rubber gloves and almost make a jokey comment about doctors and sex, but think better of it. Time and place, after all.

The tattoo needle starts to buzz and all I feel is a light tingle, not the pain I was expecting. I wouldn't say it's relaxing, but it's not painful either. Matt talks to me throughout, mostly about the music that's playing over the sound system. It seems we have very similar taste in music. I'm unfamiliar with the band that is playing, Staind, and look them up on iTunes using my phone. Before the album has finished I've downloaded it. I lose track of time, and I guess we've gone through at least three different albums when Matt finally sits back and the noise of the gun stops.

'It's done,' he tells me. I can hear the pride in his work through his voice.

I can't wait to see it, suddenly realizing how much faith I've placed in a stranger. He could have tattooed anything on my back, and it's permanent.

When I look in the mirror's reflection, I can't help the grin that lights up my face, I absolutely love it. The tattoo and surrounding area are red, but you can still see the detail shine through.

Matt asks me to lie back down so he can put some Hustle Butter on the tattoo. Apparently it's the best product to encourage healing and prevent scabbing. When he shows me the tub it looks a little like a solid wax. I rub some between my fingers and it melts. It's a lovely texture and fragrance. Matt gently massages the butter onto my tattoo. He has amazing hands, even with the gloves on. His touch not only heats my skin, it wakes up my sex drive, and it's so sensual.

I hear the gloves being removed and tossed into the bin, but before I can get up, Matt's hands have returned. If I thought it felt good before, it's heaven now.

He caresses the area outside my fresh ink, moving closer to my ass cheeks, which are partly on display to allow access for the tattoo. His hands make a trail up and down my spine, followed by gentle kisses that perfectly mimic his movements. I should be shocked, but right now I'm enjoying it far too much to complain.

I feel the gentle tug of my skirt and pants being pulled down, leaving my ass on full display. I'm about to protest when Matt shushes me.

'Just go with it, Alice. You know you want to.' Hell yes, I want to.

'But..' I'm about to ask him why; he's half my age, after all. What can he possibly see in me? His lips touch my ass cheek so softly that I sharply draw in a breath. I yelp when he nips me with his teeth. His hand soothes the area where he's bitten, a gentle circular motion, and then there's a loud slap and my ass is on fire. Holy shit! I'm shocked, but so turned on.

I try to turn my head, but Matt tells me to stay exactly where I am. All the while his hands are touching and exploring my lower body, and it seems rather rude of me to ignore him, so I do as I'm told.

His firm hands part my legs a little, and then his finger flicks against my clit. I almost fall off the bed when I jump at the shock of it. Matt soothes me again and then proceeds to rotate my clit with his fingers. My body feels like its going to explode, sensations are overwhelming me.

I hear the sound of a zipper being lowered and I'm drawn down the table towards him. My legs are opened a little wider and I feel the head of his cock rubbing against my clit. Fireworks are about to go off behind my eyes.

'Holy shit!' I scream, as his cock enters my very wet pussy.

He thrusts deeply, and then pulls out almost fully. He repeats this a few times until I'm begging him for release. He rotates his hips and I lose myself in an orgasm. Before I've even come down he's fucking me with everything he's got, and boy has he got it. He hits all the right spots; his cock feels like an iron rod, slamming in and out of me. He's got some stamina, that's for sure.

A second orgasm rolls over me, just as I hear a loud grunt from Matt. 'Fuck, yeah!' he shouts as the warmth of his own release fills me. Bloody hell, that's the best sex I've ever had, I totally love this growing old disgracefully.

I'm rudely brought back from my fantasy when I feel the lukewarm coffee spilling on my lap. I was so lost in my adventure that I forgot I was holding it. Yuck. I save the word document before I go clean myself up, hoping that I'm half as lucky with my own tattoo experience next week.

The tattoo shop looks exactly like I imagined it from the outside; of course, I've seen pictures of it.

The inside is slightly gloomy and there's a chill in the air, the sun outside unable to penetrate the tinting on the window. I'm disappointed to see that the tattoo chair doesn't look like a bed at all, just a padded chair in a semi reclined position.

There's a tired black leather sofa sitting in front of the window, and a stereo at the side blasting out rock music. It's Five Finger Death Punch and one of my favorites 'House of the rising sun'. The shop front is empty so I take a moment to look around. There are pencil sketches on the walls portraying a variety of tattoos; it's an eclectic mix of fairies, dragons, and skulls. The artist's skill shining through in all of them.

Matt walks through from the back and I almost giggle. He looks nothing like my fantasy. He's shorter than me by a good few inches and I'm only five foot seven. He definitely doesn't have a six pack, instead sporting a small paunch that doesn't look too dissimilar to my own flabby belly, and he's almost my age. His hair is thinning at the front, and he's tried to disguise it with a buzz cut. There's absolutely no spark there whatsoever. I'm kind of relieved.

Matt greets me warmly; even his voice is different. It's higher pitched than my fantasy Matt, there's almost a girlish lilt to it. He shows me to the sofa, offering me a seat. Matt sits down next to me and hands me a piece of paper. Now this is something that does match my vision. It's the tattoo, and it's perfect. The detail on the design shows off every curve of the skull, even the shading that makes the design pop. The lettering is cursive but legible, and snakes around the top and bottom of the image.

Matt asks me to lower the top of my skirt so he can apply the template. Luckily, I'd worn my elastic waisted skirt to make this bit easier, not to mention it's one of the few skirts I own that makes me feel thin. I'd paired it with a strappy black vest and heels. I may not feel confident, but at least I looked it.

That's where we hit a problem. Apparently there's a curve in my spine. Funny that, I thought everyone has a curve in their spine, but apparently not. What this means is that the template doesn't sit right on my back. Matt gives it a moment's thought then pulls up a normal kitchen chair. He asks me to sit back to front with my legs astride the black and chrome chair. My chest is resting against the back, stretching my spine out. He applies a second template and pronounces that one as perfect. Relief floods through me. Having waited this long to get a tattoo, for a moment there, I thought it wasn't going to happen.

In this position my ass isn't quite as visible as I'd imagined, thankfully, as not long after we've started, the shop door opens and a guy walks in.

Unfortunately, because of the way I'm leaning over the top of the chair this new arrival gets a full on view of my ample cleavage. There's nothing I can do to cover myself up.

The new guy plonks himself on the sofa, his eyes affixed to my boobs. He splays his legs and makes himself comfortable; it looks like he's settling in for the duration. He opens the fridge next to the sofa and pull out a beer; he's obviously familiar with the place. The cheeky sod could have offered me the ice cold can of Coke that was sat next to it. The interior of the shop suddenly seems to have become uncomfortably warm.

What follows is two hours of hell. It's not the tattoo, that's fine. The needle feels more like tiny scratches and tickles; even the part right on top of my spine is nothing more than mild discomfort. The problem is the conversation the guys have over my head, apparently oblivious to my presence. By the time Matt sits back and tells me he's finished the tattoo, I've heard more than I ever wanted to know about both their sex lives, especially the dirty blonde that the new guy had sex with all last night. I need bleach for my mind, and he definitely needs bleach for his bed sheets. When he said dirty he didn't mean kinky. Eurgh. He treated us to a blow-by-blow account of his evening, from her arrival to her departure. I'm not even sure he knows her name. I cringe. I may write erotic fiction, but this sounds more like the plot of a bad porno movie.

Matt goes through the motions, explaining what he's doing as he massages the Hustle Butter into my tattoo. When his latex clad fingers touch my skin there's no reaction. My eyes almost pop when he pulls out a box of cling film. He wraps it around my mid riff and I feel like a trussed up turkey. Matt explains that I need to keep it on for an hour or so, just to protect the tattoo. I hurriedly pull my skirt up and my top down, trying to restore some semblance of order to my clothing.

Matt seems happy to chat forever, but I feel so uncomfortable I push him to complete the transaction. I hand over the cash, reassuring Matt that I love my new ink. I absolutely adore it and can't wait to show it off. I've already posted the photo he took on my phone for me to Facebook.

Throwing a quick goodbye over my shoulder, I rush from the shop and back to the safety of my car.

Granted, it wasn't the experience I'd imagined, but the thrill of my new tattoo makes it all worthwhile, and who knows, perhaps I'll even get a story out of dirty blonde sex one day!

Chapter Thirteen — Bruises

Now I've got my tattoo, it's time to take the next step in my delayed youth rebellion. I write about hot Australian bikers, but the truth is I know nothing about motorbikes. I can probably count on one hand how many times I've been on the back of a bike, and that was so long ago it was before I passed my car test. Since driving a car I seem to have an abnormal fear of two wheels. In the interests of book research it's time to do something about that. Have you ever heard of a biker chick that was scared of bikes? Exactly.

I've booked my motorbike test today. It's just a simple competency test following a few hours of being taught the basics. If, no, *when* I pass I'll be able to ride a 125cc bike.

I haven't had the best nights sleep, but at least when I wake up it's a dry day, albeit there's a chill in the air. It's October after all so I guess I should be grateful it's not pissing it down like it normally does on a weekend.

I don my chunky ankle boots, jeans and a warm top. The bike school is lending me the rest of the kit I need to wear, as well as the bike.

I park my trusty, safe, four-wheeled car in the school playground and walk around the corner to see a row of two-wheeled nemesis facing me.

I'm not sure what brought about this fear; it certainly wasn't getting knocked off my bicycle at eleven by a minibus and bouncing across the road on my knees. I carried on cycling from one side of town to the other for a good few years still. I can only think it was the realization of how lucky I was to be alive.

Once I learned how to drive a car I finally understood just quite how dangerous many of the maneuvers I'd performed on that bicycle had been. I'd cycled down the side of buses, into the blind spots of lorries and even used to cycle to school with a guitar dangling from the handlebars.

Other than the accident with the minibus I think my most interesting incident had been falling off the bicycle in front of a policeman whilst trying to cycle home with a wooden pasteboard. To the policeman's disgust my mothers opening phrase had been concern for the pasteboard instead of her daughter.

Come to think of it, that had been the same when I told her the minibus had hit me. She was more worried about the state of the bicycle than me. That could explain why I'm a bit of a tough cookie. If you fell over in my house you just picked yourself up and got on with it.

The instructors I've chosen have an excellent reputation in the local area, and they insist on supplying the correct equipment to keep you safe, so really I should have nothing to worry about. But then again, we are talking about me.

I'm a bag of nerves as I walk up to one of the instructors and announce my presence. To my disappointment none of them look like the bikers from my books. There's a distinct lack of black leather for a start, they're wearing chunky, warm textile jackets with fluorescent safety vests.

The protective gear they offer me doesn't live up to expectation either. I don the oversized jacket, which suddenly makes me look twenty pounds heavier than I am. The gloves are so well worn they have holes in the inside lining which is a touch uncomfortable, and they make my hands feel heavy and clumsy. Come to think of it that's how I feel all over once I'm fully equipped and kitted out.

There are only three of us in this particular class, and I'm by far the oldest. Looking at the instructor I'm probably old enough to be his mother. The other two candidates look so young I'm surprised they're old enough to take their test. So now, not only do I feel nervous, I feel ancient as well.

The instructor begins by introducing us to the bikes we'll be riding. It's a mix of a safety briefing and a beginners guide to what makes a bike work and some tips on maintenance. They've given me a 125cc black motorbike and the boys are given push and go mopeds. Before we're allowed to start we have to answer questions on what we've just been told. I'm looking at the bike in front of me wondering how I'll ever get my head around the front brake not being a brake, but a clutch. As a cyclist that handle stops the front wheel, apparently on a motorbike it performs a different function. Who knew? I can see plenty of bruises in my immediate future.

The first test is to be able to put the bike on the kickstand, and then take it off again. The first attempt goes well. The second time I totally forget what I was told and almost end up wearing the bike. After a few more failures the instructor suggests that I may want to start off with a moped instead. I reluctantly agree. Better to get the hang of two wheels in its simplest form for now.

We spend the morning riding round the school playground, around traffic cones that are supposed to represent the road. I'm not a fan of right turns but find I can handle left.

The moped feels like it's racing along. I'm told that at my fastest I'm doing around 10-15mph and encouraged to speed up. Eek.

We break for lunch after which we're told we'll have another hours practice then we're off on the open road. The instructor sees the look of panic on my face and assures me that he wouldn't let me loose on the road if he didn't believe I wasn't capable. That does nothing to reassure me.

Lunch is a quiet affair of hot dogs and mugs of tea in a garage full of bike gear. A few of the other classes have joined us, and I've still to see a single biker that looks anything like I imagined. There's a mix of large and small, short and tall with very little leather in sight. My libido is so disappointed she's buggered off for the day and left me to it. I can't say I blame her really.

One of the boys doesn't return after lunch, so the instructor leads the two of us that remain on to the main road.

Whilst the school playground, with its traffic cone markers, seemed a little restrictive, the thought of the roads with real traffic bring a lump to my throat.

The wind is blowing against us and the road is full of potholes. Whilst this road wouldn't be an issue in the car, it's not one I'm comfortable tackling on two wheels. It's a country lane with barely enough room for two cars to pass side by side, and busier than I expected. It feels like there's constantly a car sat behind us waiting to overtake. I can imagine the curses coming from the drivers who rush by impatiently as soon as a gap appears. Let's face it; if I were one of them the air would be blue in my car.

I breathe a sigh of relief when we turn off the road into a trading estate and park up for a break. I'm not sure it's an official break as much as an excuse for the instructor to sneak a cigarette.

Pulling the glove off my left hand I'm horrified to see it's snapped one of my lovely long nails. So much for protective clothing. I'm rather traumatized at breaking a nail, I'd just got them all to the right length and now I'll have to cut them all short to match. Did I mention it's broken that low down it's almost to the core.

Apparently the trading estate has been chosen as a quiet place to practice our turn in the road. This proves to be something that was much easier to perform in a school playground without the real barrier of kerbs.

In hindsight I suspect part of the problem was lack of speed, combined with a failure to turn my head in the direction I wanted the moped to go. My gaze seemed to be locked on the kerb directly ahead of me, and like a car crash waiting to happen; I know this is not going to end well. It doesn't.

Moments later I'm in a heap on the road with a moped on top of me. The shock of the whole thing means that it takes a moment for me to realize that it hurts. The next realization is that I don't think I can lift the moped up and off me from this angle. Luckily I don't have to. The poor instructor rushes over to assist. His face is a mask of panic. Whilst my concern is that I haven't damaged the bike, he's worrying about me. I brush him off. I'm fine. There's no tear in the leg of my jeans although I suspect I'll have a nice bruise by the time we get back. I'm still more concerned about the broken nail from earlier rather than any other damage I may have inflicted.

I'm sent to a nearby car park, which is the same width as the road, to practice my turn. Without a kerb to distract me I achieve perfect turns every time. Go figure.

The rest of the examination passes without incident. A few times the instructors voice comes through the headset asking me to speed up but other than that I'm doing it, even if I don't feel an ounce of confidence. The whole ride I've been a bag of nerves.

When we get back I'm presented with a shiny certificate and a promise that if I return they will instill confidence in me. It's what they do. They're a great bunch of guys and I believe that if anyone can make me feel safe on a bike it would be them.

The young boy who took his lesson with me asks for directions to the bus stop. I offer him a lift into town. The 30mph drive feels so slow compared to the moped I feel sure I could walk faster. The bike at this speed felt more like 60mph.

As I wave goodbye after dropping off my fellow biker (how good does it feel to say that!), I notice an amber light on the dashboard. This doesn't look good. It's a warning light for the engine. I'm sure my car is throwing a tantrum at the thought of being replaced. It needn't have worried; I no longer have plans to purchase a motorbike of my own in my immediate future.

A trip to the garage on the way home quickly dissipates any pleasure I had from passing my test. It's not good news. I'm looking at a repair bill costing several hundred pounds. I'm definitely not going to be buying a bike any time soon, even if I'd wanted to.

Once home I gingerly remove my jeans to inspect the damage. There's a huge lump on my leg and it's already multi colored. A long soak in the bath does little to ease the stiffness and ache that has settled in my leg.

By the following morning I look like I have a third arse cheek. The swelling and bruising are pretty impressive if I do say so myself.

Only I could go for a motorbike lesson and end up falling off. No sign of any hot bikers in black leather, indeed the only black in sight is the mottled bruising on my leg.

One day Alice, one day you'll get to live out a fantasy rather than a fiasco.

Chapter Fourteen – The

Dating Site

Having found that active participation in book research isn't such a good idea I should have known better than to attempt it again.

Research should be restricted to Google; after all it has the answer to any question you can think of and then some. But no. This is me we're talking about. Hence I embark on my next disaster all in the name of story research.

One of the stories I am writing has a journalist investigating dating sites and cheating. Encouraged by my friend I sign up.

I have no wish to meet anyone. I'm newly single and happily so. I'm pretty sure that I'll be happy with that status for the rest of my life.

Having answered what feels like a million questions at sign up my account is live. I'm confused when I see the suggestions before me. When my friend showed me the site the other day it was full of attractive and interesting looking guys. At this point I should probably mention that my friend is ten years younger than me. What I've just been presented with looks like a cross between a police most wanted list and a high school yearbook full of nerds.

Despite carefully entering my parameters the site has seen fit to present me with a bunch of old men. Not only are they old men, they are sad old men. After an evening of responding to messages in my inbox I'm forced to conclude that they are desperate, sad old men. I feel unclean after reading some of the messages that were sent to me.

An icon pops up in the corner of the screen and curiosity has me opening the senders' profile. For Gods sake – he's an 18 year old offering a very blatant sex only hook up. I'm old enough to be his mother!

I shut the site down, not sure it's actually going to help me write the book I'm working on. My friend is coming over tomorrow, I'll chat it over with her.

Laura is laughing at me. I've told her about the contacts I've had on the dating site.

'To be fair what I really wanted to write was a scene where she comes across her best friends husband on the site.' I tell her.

My plan had been that the investigative journalist finds her best friends husband on the site, and realizes that he's cheating on his wife. Unable to keep her friend in the dark she tells the friend, the marriage breaks up and the husband comes after the journalist, seeking revenge.

Laura and I are chatting about the plot when she suddenly gasps. When I ask her what's wrong she points to the image on the screen in front of her.

It's her friends' husband, using an assumed name. See, I knew this kind of thing happened!

After discussing it we decide she should send him a message, feigning innocence and asking if he'd forgotten he still had the account.

Five minutes later he's blocked her and I'm resolved to write the story line after all.

A few weeks later, having finished writing my book I'd forgotten all about the dating site until an email popped up to tell me I had unread messages.

Curiosity got the better of me and I logged on. The first few messages were more of the same old rubbish. They're full of guys looking for everlasting love and happy ever after. Thanks, but no thanks.

I paused over the delete button on one message. My gut said no, but my head said why not. It was a guy who'd lost his wife a few years ago and was younger than me. He looked okay; unlike many he was literate in his message. I figured it wouldn't hurt to meet for a drink as we had a few interests in common. A bit of company down the pub would make a nice change. It can be quite lonely being an author working at home.

We arranged to meet up in the local pub one weekday afternoon. It was within walking distance so I could have a drink, and as it was mid afternoon there was no pressure.

I arrived early so settled in the lounge bar with a Jack Daniels. Every time a guy walked in on his own I checked him out. Nope. Not the guy I was supposed to be meeting.

I looked up when my name was called to find a stranger in front of me. This was my date? His profile photo must have been at least ten years old. He had hair in his photo for a start and bore no resemblance to the man in front of me.

We struggled through a conversation for the next hour; it was full of uncomfortable pauses. I don't think we actually had anything in common after all.

Where he'd said he liked the same things as me it was apparent now that he didn't.

I felt awful when I made up an appointment I had to leave for, and he asked if we could meet up again. There was no chance of that happening. I said I'd let him know. All the way home I tried to think of a dignified, but gentle way of saying 'no chance'.

Some time later I received a message from someone on the dating site asking why they hadn't been good enough for me to contact them. I didn't know that by paying a subscription for the site you could see who had viewed your profile. I'd looked at this particular guys profile but quickly discarded it as he was much shorter than me, and I'm a girl who likes to wear heels.

I decided honesty was the best policy and told him so. A new message pinged on my inbox. He was persistent; I'd give him that.

I opened the message and ended up playing message ping-pong with him for most of the day. It was quite obvious all he was after was a hook up. I'd been stood up on a couple of dates that I'd organized through the site, so appreciated his bluntness.

Reminding myself that I was an erotic author who should take chances, I agreed to meet up. Nothing was promised.

I was nervous as hell. It was over twenty five years since I'd dated, and that had been very infrequent. I'd met my husband through friends. I'd no memory of how dating worked, and I'd never done hook ups, so this was new territory for me. I was definitely out of my comfort zone.

He was charming, had a killer smile (my weakness) and he made me laugh. It turns out we grew up around the corner from each other, although he was a number of years younger than me. Conversation was easy and flowed, but I was still a bag of nerves.

I decided what the hell. It was time to live like an erotic author not a church mouse.

There are times in life when you should say what you think. There are also times in life when you should most definitely keep your mouth shut and your opinions to yourself.

Unfortunately, when you find yourself in a situation that shocks the hell out of you, it's not always easy to remember that.

When presented with an erection that required a magnifying glass to find it, I'm guessing that an appropriate response shouldn't have been a very shocked and disgusted 'Is that it?'

What I do know is that I should have walked out then and there. Sadly, I discovered that size *is* important, and that it's not what you do with it. It was so quick that I'm pretty sure I now know what it would be like to be with a teenage boy. Wham, bam thank you ma'am and no thought to whether I enjoyed it or not. Guess that's Karma's way of telling me off for speaking my mind.

I went home determined to cancel my dating site membership. The life of a church mouse suddenly seemed enticing.

Chapter Fifteen – Santa's

Helper

Christmas Eve

I pause the video on Facebook and reach for a tissue. Deep down I'm a big softie and watching that short clip has made me misty eyed. I'm also a sucker for a good-looking guy so I can't resist hitting the play button again.

The screen shows a moonlit street, the ghostly shadows of suburban houses in the background. The roar of approaching motorbikes breaks the tranquility. A cavalcade of bikers comes into view; polished chrome reflects the Christmas lights and tinsel decorating the bikes and the riders are decked out in festive costumes.

Scrolling text tells the story of an MC who gives out gifts at Christmas to children in need, be that poverty, illness, disability, or they've lost a parent. Tiny faces light up with joy at receiving gifts that range from dolls and teddy bears to trikes and leather cuts. Carers or parents look on with grateful, teary eyes. That sets my own eyes watering again. I quickly dab them with the tissue just in time for my video highlight to appear on screen.

He's gorgeous! Tall, tattooed, just a hint of stubble gracing his chiseled features and by far the sexiest Santa lookalike I've ever seen. I'm pretty sure the improper thoughts he brings to mind have put me on top of Santa's naughty list.

His voice is deep and gravelly and just hearing it has me melting. I'd like to sit on his knee!

The clip comes to an end too quickly, freezing on the frame showing my sexy Santa. I'm torn between hitting the play button again, or just sitting here ogling his fine physique. It's no good, I've got work to do, a story to be written.

I dunk the last chocolate digestive in my coffee, savoring the melted chocolate as much as the image on the screen in front of me. As I wipe the crumbs from my lip I'm already locking myself out of Facebook and setting the timer on the program that will keep me locked out for the next few hours so I can concentrate on my manuscript.

Word opens up, the flashing cursor taunting me over my lack of words. My muse appears to be missing in action so I do the next best thing. I fantasize about the sexy Santa instead.

The roar of the bike seems to stop outside my house. I can't think of anyone in the cul-de-sac that would know any bikers, I'm well into my prime but I'm still the youngest resident. Curiosity gets the better of me and I sneak a peek between the slats of the blinds on the front window. A hulking bike sits at the end of the path leading to my bungalow, and there's a large figure walking down the path toward my door. I jump back, startled. What the hell?

The chime of the doorbell breaks the silence, echoing in the empty hallway. I hesitate. It's late, from the lack of lights in the windows across the street I'm guessing everyone else is already in bed for the night. Not that anyone round here would be fit enough to come and help me if I needed them. Perhaps if I ignore him he'll go away. The ticking of the clock sounds unbelievably loud, the seconds moving by slowly. The doorbell chimes again, this time it's accompanied by a loud rapping on the glass door. The glass almost rattles in the wooden frame from the impact.

"I know you're in there, you might as well open up." The voice is strong and forceful, yet I don't think I can hear any harm or malice in it. Can you hear that in a voice? I begin to doubt my own reasoning even as I head slowly to the door.

The chain on the door is broken and I silently curse my delay in getting it repaired. Until now I've always felt safe in my own home. I hesitate with my hand on the door handle. The hallway light is off but the porch light casts a shadow of the stranger on the other side of my door. He looks scarily large. Taking in a deep breath for courage I open the door just a little, peeking through the gap. Whoever this stranger is he's stood with his back to me.

"Hello?" There's a quiver in my voice as I speak. The stranger moves to face me.

I'm pretty sure my jaw drops as his face is revealed in the dull light of the porch. He looks like a film star or a book cover model. He's bloody gorgeous! The rugged looks are out of sync with his outfit; he's *dressed like a sexy Santa. I can see enough to tell that this isn't some cheap costume from Amazon. The polished leather of his belt and boots, and the burnished brass of the buttons reflect the light.*

He smiles and I feel myself go weak at the knees. I grasp the doorframe for support and unconsciously allow the door to creak open a little further.

"I'm looking for Alice."

"And you are?" Part of me wants to shout out loud that I'm Alice, but a tiny part of me begs for restraint and caution. There's something odd about this whole situation. It's surreal finding myself talking to a hunky Santa, especially here on my own doorstep.

"I'm Santa's helper." He grins. "I've got a package for you." I can't help myself, no sooner has he uttered the words than my eyes are checking out his groin. Is that? No, it can't be. I'm sure it is

though. The heavy material is tenting with what can only be a massive erection. Holy crap.

A polite cough draws my attention back to sexy Santa's face. Shit! He knows exactly where my eyes were focused and he's laughing at me. I can feel the heat of embarrassment flushing my cheeks. I'm trying to stutter out an apology when he reaches into his trouser pocket and pulls out a large gift-wrapped box. Glancing down, I'm almost disappointed to realize that's what was filling his trousers.

"Santa couldn't find you on his naughty list this year so he's sent you a little something to help you be a touch naughtier." The sexy stranger gives me a panty-wetting grin as he hands the gift over. "Christmas only comes once a year," he smiles, "And Santa thought you should at least match it."

I'm mortified. How the fuck does he know I've not had an orgasm in over a year? Has he been reading my books?

My mouth is moving but nothing's coming out. I'm literally at a loss for words. My hand instinctively reaches for the parcel, but sexy Santa doesn't completely release it.

"Santa sent me along to help you out." He winks at me. "Just in case you've forgotten how to use this." He finally releases the present. Can you believe the audacity of this guy? Still, there's something about him that prevents me from shutting the door. I'm not sure if its presence, charisma, or I've just totally lost my mind, but I step back and gesture for him to enter.

His large frame fills my hallway, I feel dwarfed in his shadow. It's not just his height; he's solidly built as well. "Can I get you a drink?" I offer, my manners overcoming my nerves.

"I'll take a Fireball please." He pauses, "Neat." He adds just as I step toward the kitchen. Where has this guy come from? He's like every sexual fantasy

I've ever had rolled up into one. And who else knows that I drink Fireball?

I must be dreaming, I decide. It's Christmas Eve and I've obviously had one too many drinks. If that's the case then I might as well roll with it, it's the best dream I've had in ages and the only action I'll have seen all year. The realization that this must be a dream releases me from my nerves and inhibitions, still I down a shot of Fireball before quickly refilling my glass and heading back to sexy Santa who I find lounging comfortably on my sofa.

It might be my home yet it's sexy Santa who pats the seat, inviting me to join him. It's a large sofa and I sit myself at the other end, leaving plenty of space. The gift he brought is on the center cushion, a safety barrier between us. I may have accepted that this is a dream, but I can't totally shed my prudish inhibitions.

"Aren't you going to open your gift?"

I look at the present, wary of it. It's an innocent looking box, it's about the length and breadth of a bottle of whisky in a gift box. I reach for it hesitantly. I'm deceived by the size as it weighs much less than a bottle. The gift wrap is an expensive looking foil with a subtle festive printed greeting. Whoever wrapped it has done a lovely job; swirling ribbons finish it off.

Teasing open one end leaves me no wiser. It's a clear plastic case but a plain cardboard wrapping obscures the gift within. "Just tear it open" he laughs. It's not in my nature to tear off the wrap.

I draw in a hiss of breath when the gift reveals itself. It's a rabbit vibrator. I'm not sure whether to be pleased, as it's a decent quality, or shocked that someone would offer me one as a gift, not to mention he's suggested he should remind me how to use it.

Part of me feels a little disappointment. As much as I know I'll enjoy my gift, I kind of wish the sexy guy beside me had been my gift instead.

"Erm, thank you, erm, I mean thank Santa for me." I stumble over the words. My manners are at war with my libido.

Santa's helper gives me a devilish grin and winks at me. "Aren't you going to try it then?" He smirks as he passes over a pack of Duracell batteries. A large pack of batteries when I'm pretty sure only two are required.

I feel the blush warm my face. This dream feels too real. I don't feel like Alice the author right currently; I feel like Alice the lonely singleton that's past her prime. I'm out of my depth and my nerves are shot.

He takes the pack of batteries from my shaking hand and replaces them with the glass of Fireball. As I take a mouthful of burning Dutch courage he's already removed the vibrator from the box and inserted the AA's. I almost drop my drink when he twists the base and a powerful thrumming noise fills the room. Wow, that's impressive. He fingers the tiny buttons on the base and I see the Rabbit's ears move independently of the body of the vibrator. Another button reverses the direction. He turns to me, grinning. "Shall we?"

"Shall we what?" I splutter a mouthful of Fireball at him. That's so unladylike of me, but I can't help it. If he'd offered me sex I'd have probably already had his trousers off by now, but asking me to use a sex toy in front of him? My inner prude is so shocked she's almost left the building!

"Relax Alice." His voice soothes me at the same time his warm hand caresses my arm. His touch is electric. I wonder why, knowing this is a dream; I'm being so reserved.

Sod it, I tell myself. Time to call on my inner whore instead.

He pushes me back against the large sofa, so I'm lying down. Slowly, he raises my long skirt, his fingers trailing lazy circles against the skin of my legs as he moves up my body. I close my eyes reveling in the sensation of his touch. His hand clasps the waistband of my knickers and teases them down. My hips rise of their own accord, assisting him. I'm so glad he's not ripping my knickers off, I'm sick of reading that in books. I silently chastise myself for thinking about anything to do with books whilst this hot guy is caressing my lower body, setting it on fire.

His finger brushes against my clit and I almost take off. I'm already sensitive and so ready for whatever else he's planning. My mind may be prone to prudish outbursts but my body is more than willing to participate.

My ears pick up the low buzz of the vibrator coming to life, moments before he strokes the head of it against me. The tension has me wanting more, needing more. "Please," I beg, not quite sure what

I'm asking for. I feel the welcome push of the vibrator's head inside me, gently pulsing as he moves it slowly in and out, going deeper on each push. That feels sooo good. The rabbit ears catch against my clit and I almost explode, sensation flooding my body, quickly followed by an orgasm that leaves me gasping for breath. Shit. I guess it has been a while. I'm mortified that I've come so quickly.

"Wow, I wasn't expecting it to work quite that well," he laughs. I strain to hear any disappointment in his words – does he mean that in a good way, or not? He reaches for my hand, drawing it towards his groin and placing it on the impressive hardness hiding under the fabric. Wow. I realize I'm a greedy girl. Not satisfied with the orgasm I've already had, I want more. I want him.

When he releases my hand I use it to loosen the ties holding the red Santa trousers up, then reach inside and grasp him. His cock fills my hand with heat and if feels silky smooth as I massage its length. He's rock hard. He stands quickly and I lose my hold on him. Disappointment floods me at the thought of not getting to experience his magnificent cock. I needn't have worried. He pulls me off the sofa and guides me around the side of it. Pushing me gently over the arm of the sofa he lifts my skirt above my waist before dropping his trousers to his ankles. One hand gently massages the base of my back whilst I'm sure his other fists his cock. He rubs his cock against my clit, mimicking his earlier movements with the vibrator, teasing me. Just as I'm about to complain he thrusts into me, slamming my hips against the solid arm of the sofa. It's hard and fast, and feels like he's trying to break me, but it's so good I'm not going to complain. I'm enjoying this far too much. The height of the sofa means his cock is hitting me at just the right angle and as I lose myself in another orgasm I'm rewarded with his loud, guttural groan signaling he's coming with me.

That was amazing. I may be a writer, but right now I can't find words to describe just how hot the whole *experience was. I'm still laid over the sofa arm, catching my breath, when I realize he's not only pulled out, he's dressed and ready to go.*

Disappointment fills me, and it's obviously written all over my face.

"I'm sorry, Alice," there's a genuine hint of regret in his voice. "That was amazing. It wasn't supposed to happen, I couldn't help myself," He said. "It's Christmas Eve and I've still got a lot of deliveries to make." He places a chaste kiss on my cheek, and before I've managed to rearrange my clothes I hear the click of the front door closing.

I sit back from the computer and can feel the sadness flowing from the screen. This isn't like my normal writing. It felt so real this time, and the loss is tangible. I close the lid of the laptop gently and decide to call it a night. It's after midnight anyway so technically it's already Christmas Day.

My brother and his family called earlier, their flight was cancelled so they won't make it after all. I look at the gifts under the tree, wrapped and waiting for my niece and nephew. The turkey was already defrosted and prepped. I'm not sure I want to cook a Christmas dinner for one. Between the disappointment I still feel from the writing and the loneliness I'm feeling at spending Christmas on my own, I think it's time for bed. With any luck I'll dream of my sexy biker again.

I stir, looking at the clock. It's three AM. I'm not sure what's woken me; I just sense that something has. I listen carefully. There's movement in the house, it's more than the crack of the heating system I'm sure. Part of me says to call the police, but part of me says there's nothing there, I'm just imagining it. The police have got better things to do than come check out phantom noises for some author with an overactive imagination.

I get out of bed as stealthily as I can. The bedroom door isn't fully closed and I stand there listening. I really must learn to check I've locked the door before I go to bed. Another noise has the hairs rising on my arms. It's coming from the front room. There's nothing to hand to protect myself with, so I just let my anger take over and start walking the few steps from the bedroom to the front room, slamming the door wide as I enter.

There's a shriek of terror as a figure rises from the foot of my Christmas tree and I almost wet myself in fear. Instead I flip the light switch at the side of the door, filling the room with bright artificial light. There's a guy dressed head to toe in black filling a bin bag with the presents from under my tree.

I'm outraged! "What the fuck do you think you're doing?" I screech.

I'm lost for words when the figure in front of me sinks to the floor and starts sobbing an apology.

Throwing caution aside I move closer. I'm out of my depth here, but I'm pretty sure this isn't how burglars normally react.

Fifteen minutes later I'm sat on the floor at the side of my burglar, patting him on the back and telling him everything's going to be okay. I haven't called the police; instead I've just offered to make him coffee. I swear, you couldn't make my life up some days and this is one of them.

My burglar is Keith, who lives just a few doors down the street from me. He's actually a pretty decent guy who's just been made redundant and couldn't face telling his two young kids that Santa wasn't coming this year. We laugh at how bad a burglar he is, as he certainly wasn't stealthy or silent, the fact he woke me says it all. I could normally sleep through a herd of rampaging elephants once I'm out.

I look at the tree, look at Keith, then make what I'm sure is a pretty stupid decision, but it's Christmas and I'm a sucker for a sob story. I invite Keith and his family to Christmas dinner. Going into my office I return with a pack of unused gift labels and proceed to replace the labels on the gifts under the tree, marking them with the name of his kids instead of my niece and nephew. It just happens his kids are the same ages. Somehow, as nonsensical as the whole situation is, it just feels right.

Several hours later I'm sitting at the dinner table, surrounded by Keith and his family. They're smiling and happy and I realize that this is what Christmas is really about. It's not the gifts under the tree, it's the day itself, spending it with other people, sharing and caring.

As much as I missed my family, I know I'll get to do a second Christmas with them next week. When I go to sleep that night I dream of my sexy biker. Christmas really was a special day.

Chapter Sixteen – An Unexpected Threesome

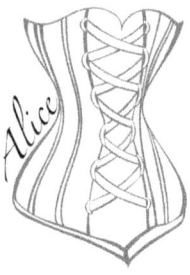

I was in my early forties before I started reading erotic fiction, if you don't count Jackie Collins or Jilly Cooper that I had last read in my late teens. One of the genres that appealed to me was M.C. I remember the first M.C book vividly, I lay there reading it and thinking that I should be disgusted by the language or appalled by the characters actions. I wasn't. I loved that book, and from that point I've embraced the genre, I'd say it also gave me an introduction to the darker stories that I love as well.

I grew up devouring Agatha Christie, Readers Digest condensed books that were full of mystery, crime and intrigue, and pretty much anything I could pick up from the local discount bookstore. I love a story that has a twist that I didn't see coming, or a crime where I can't guess whodunnit. At my lowest point emotionally I was reading around 400 books a year. The introduction of the Kindle really transformed my life. If it hadn't been for Kindle and the new indie authors that I discovered through it, I wouldn't have found the courage to change my life, become an author myself or set up a book signing from scratch.

For many readers a book is just a temporary pleasure, something to enjoy for a few hours then put down and get back on with life. For others, and I know because I was one, it's a necessary escape. Life in reality is so unpleasant or uncomfortable that a book transports you away from that. I've always preferred a good book to a movie. There's so much more detail in a book; couple that with your own imagination and you're in an alternate reality.

Books can make us laugh out loud, make us cry or scare the crap out of us. A really great book has a little bit of everything in it. It takes you on an emotional journey and leaves you exhausted and wrung out when you finish it. With a book it's so much easier to picture yourself as one of the characters. There's no comparing yourself to a stick thin actress. In a book nothing is impossible. I've even read a ghost book that left me too scared to go to the bathroom on my own. Imagination is a powerful thing, and books are a fantastic illustration of that.

But I digress. My love of M.C. meant that I was introduced to the concept of a threesome. A ménage if you will, but it was so vivid and dirty that I found myself engrossed. I've read many more books that contained multiple partners, but none has affected me quite as much as that first scene.

I'm sitting at my desk contemplating writing a threesome, but it's so far from my realm that I'm not sure I could do it justice. Do I write MMF or MFF?

Whilst I've nothing against the MFF scenes I've read, some have been pretty hot; I think for me the preference would be MMF.

The problem before me is that a couple of the scenes I've read have been so good; I don't feel I could possibly do them justice. How's that for a confession. I have found a limit. Of course I don't write BDSM either, if you don't know the scene fully then it shows. I leave that to the amazing Tiffany Reisz. An acquaintance on Twitter told me I should read The Siren. Wow. That woman is a legend. If you'd seen me screaming for joy and jumping around the room the day she replied to me on Twitter you'd have laughed. Trust me, even authors' fan girl. That woman is in a whole league of her own, and yes, she's written some pretty powerful threesomes as well.

The phone rings and reluctantly pulls me from the party going on in my imagination. Damn, I was quite enjoying that visual. It's my brother.

"Hi, Alice." He greets me in the tone of voice that tells me he's about to ask a favor.

My brother reminds me of Del Boy in Only Fools and Horses. He's a lot younger than Del Boy, but there's some part of his character that brings to mind the hapless Del, in a good way of course. He mimics some of the characters phrases on occasion, and bears a passing resemblance to him as well. Not to mention we both think that 'this time next year we'll be millionaires.' Well, a girl can dream.

"How's everyone?" I ask, trying to delay the inevitable request.

"Good, good. Look, I hate to ask, but…" I told you. I saw that one coming as soon as I picked up the phone.

"Any chance you could babysit for us tonight?" My mum and brother are massive Elvis fans, they're attending an Elvis tribute together this evening and my poor sister in law is ill. I adore my niece and nephew so it's no hardship spending an evening in their company. I happily agree.

My mother is such a massive Elvis fan that I guess I was brainwashed on his music growing up. I was in my mid teens before I realized I could actually listen to modern music if I wanted. I actually named one of my M.C characters Elvis and had him hum my mother's favorite song 'Wonder of You', just before I killed him off! I dreaded my mother reading that scene more than the sex scenes.

I finish the call with my brother, and we agree that he'll drop the kids off in an hour so he has time to travel to the venue. That means I won't have time to write the scene I was planning after all. I need to go put some clean sheets on the guest bed before they get here.

The evening is spent playing Best of British, which they win, Monopoly that I win (I have a mean streak when it comes to games, just ask K L Shandwick and Tracie Podger what I'm like playing Trivial Pursuit), and drinking hot chocolate with cream and marshmallows cuddled together on the sofa.

It's around ten p.m. when I've finally got them tucked up in bed. There's nothing I want to watch on T.V so I decide to head to my own bed and read on my Kindle. I've got the latest Tiffany Reisz on there.

By ten thirty my Kindle is cast aside. I look at the three sets of feet protruding from the end of the quilt and sigh. I may have been fantasizing about a hot threesome earlier, but I've found myself in an altogether different threesome for the night. My niece and nephew are cuddled either side of me, snoring away happily. It may not have been the scene I envisaged, but I have to say it's sure warmed my heart.

I wouldn't have it any other way.

Chapter Seventeen — Second Chances

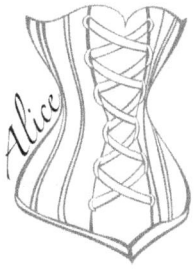

The guy from the dating site, you remember the one that was rather under endowed? Yes, him. He's been hassling me. I might have made the mistake of a second get together in the hope that it got better. It didn't. Or the third time. I guess I'm a sucker for punishment. The final straw was a jealous streak that I had mistaken for misplaced humor, when he told me I wasn't allowed to wear my new short leather skirt outside of the house. Excuse me? I thought we lived in the twenty first century, not the Middle Ages. As he had no redeeming features he had to go. To be fair even if he'd possessed any talent in the bedroom he'd still have had to go as no one gets away with telling me what I can and can't do; not even my mother. I have a tattoo to prove it.

The dating website had proved rather unremarkable to say the least. It was time to delete my profile. I'd only ever signed up for book research after all, not happy ever after. I may be the queen of online shopping, but there was nothing on the site that proved anywhere near desirable.

Tired of receiving messages from Mr. Unremarkable I opened the app, ready to find out how to cancel my account. A message had come in from someone new. If it hadn't been a Sunday morning where I had nothing better to do I'd have ignored it. Instead, armed with a hot coffee and a chocolate digestive, I clicked open.

For once I'm not met with a police mug shot or a face that would have looked better with a paper bag on it. It's a photo of a guy in a dinner jacket. I'm not sure I fancy dealing with someone posh, I'm a down to earth girl after all, but I click on reply.

I'm not quite sure how it happened, but we spent the day messaging back and forth and agreed to meet for a coffee on Thursday. Coffee sounds safe. I'm already meeting my best friend for brunch so jokingly suggest he has to get her approval first. I'm gob smacked when he agrees. We set a date for lunchtime in Costa, half an hour before my bestie is getting picked up. This way she can check him out for me, and for some reason this makes me feel a lot more comfortable about the whole thing.

I'd given up on meeting anyone, not that I wanted to in the first place. It just seemed like an opportunity to meet someone to hang out with for a drink and the theatre occasionally that presented itself whilst doing book research.

Full of cold and exhausted after working all hours to hit a deadline on a new release, I enjoyed the back and forth banter we shared over the next few days. The amount of things we had in common seemed to good to be true – music, movies, TV and even Moto GP. I actually began to think there was something off about it all.

In one conversation we were chatting about music and the subject went on to ringtones. We were trying to think of a ringtone that perfectly described us. Have you ever enjoyed a song without really listening to the lyrics? I went with a song title that I loved – Crazy Bitch by Buckcherry. A few moments later after he'd Googled the lyrics he told me what they were. I was mortified! Note to self – never, ever again suggest a song for your ringtone if you don't know the words. Luckily he couldn't see the flush of embarrassment over the phone.

Thursday arrived with a lot of trepidation. Having decided I wasn't going to do the dating thing anymore I still found myself wanting it to work. I think that was mostly down to how well we'd connected online already. What if the reality didn't live up to the expectation, not just for me, but for him as well?

Brunch was as enjoyable as always, but it seemed to speed around to lunch in no time at all. Nerves kicked in, and I found myself watching the door every time it opened. It's amazing how many guys come into Costa on their own when you're meeting a guy for the first time.

Marco arrived exactly on time, and surprised me with a box of red Lindt. He'd definitely been paying attention to our chats earlier in the week. They're my favorite chocolate. Before I knew it our time was over, and gentleman that he was, he carried my shopping for me and walked me to my bus stop. We'd both enjoyed our first meet up and arranged a date for the following night at my house. I'd cook. All the way home I kept trying to work out the catch. There had to be one, after all, all my previous online dating experiences had proved disastrous. I couldn't think of one.

The following day I was meeting up with my co-author, but if I left early enough for the drive back I'd be home in plenty of time. It was a rough journey, but luckily not as bad as some I'd endured. The motorway always seems to jam up around Doncaster, but today I'd managed to hit it quite well.

The miles seemed to fly by as I looked forward to our upcoming date. Then karma kicked in. I'm not sure what I did in a previous life to piss off karma quite so badly, but for the first time in twelve years I got a period. A bloody doubled up in agony and need to hug a hot water bottle all night period. Thankfully service stations sell Costa coffee and ibuprofen which helped me get home.

I hugged my microwaved heat bag for the rest of the afternoon, in between preparing a meal. No matter how well the date went now, it would be a chaste one. Comfortable clothes meant jeans and a sweater rather than anything sexy and revealing.

The doorbell rang and the nerves kicked in. Opening the door I was greeted by a bunch of flowers and a huge grin. I told you I was a sucker for a smile.

Of course, I could tell you how the rest of the date went, but a nice girl doesn't kiss and tell. Anyone would think I was an erotic author!

To be continued…

Acknowledgements

I couldn't have become an author without the support of my amazing readers. Thank you for taking a chance on me.

I hope that you have more Alice fantasy moments in your life than you have Alice reality experiences, and I hope that reading Alice's adventures has brought a smile to your face.

There aren't words enough to thank Tina Gephart for the difference that she made to my life; her carefully crafted words gave me hope and courage and helped me change for the better. I will forever be grateful.

About Ava Manello

Ava is a passionate reader, blogger, publisher, and author who loves nothing more than helping other Indie authors publish their books be that reviewing, beta reading, formatting or proofreading. She will always be a reader first and foremost.

She loves erotic suspense that's well written and engages the reader, and loves promoting the heck out of it for her favorite authors.

As Ava says: "I took a chance and followed a dream when I wrote my first book. It was scary, challenging and hard work, but above all it was worth it."

Stalk Ava

Facebook: www.facebook.com/avamanello

Website: http://www.avamanello.co.uk

Twitter: www.twitter.com/avamanello

Newsletter: http://eepurl.com/bb4Q4n

Goodreads: https://www.goodreads.com/author/show/7873269.Ava_Manello

Other Books by Ava Manello

Wounded Heroes Series

Declan (Wounded Heroes 1)

Cam (Wounded Heroes 2) – coming Autumn 2016

Naked Nights Series

Strip Back (Naked Nights 0.5 Eric's Story)

Strip Teaser (Naked Nights 1)

Severed MC Series

Co-authored with K. T. Fisher

Severed Angel (Severed MC 1)

Carnal Desire (Severed MC 2)

Severed Justice (Severed MC 3)

Carnal Persuasion (Severed MC 4)

Thank you for reading. I'd be really grateful if you could leave a review for the book if you have enjoyed it.